Black Petals

Black Petals

A Novel

by

Bryan Rostron

First published by Jacana Media (Pty) Ltd in 2009

10 Orange Street
Sunnyside
Auckland Park 2092
South Africa
+2711 628 3200
www.jacana.co.za

ISBN 978-1-77009-648-6

Set in Sabon 10.5/15pt
Printed by CTP Book Printers
Job No. 000926

See a complete list of Jacana titles at www.jacana.co.za

TO SUNNY

& VUYELWA

When I am sitting at the window,

Through the panes, which the snow blurs,

I think I see the image, hers,

That's not now passing ... not passing by ...

Fernando Pessoa (1888 – 1935)

One

MACAULAY Vogel stepped out of his room at the Castle. He blinked against fierce evening sunlight; sucked in hot, spicy sea air. His office was dark and smelt of mould. On the brightest day he had to work under a single bare bulb, straining to make sense of the reports. The hoard of files had been dumped carelessly by the police. In some places documents reached the low wooden ceiling. Now, mingled with that centuries' old reek of sunless damp, Vogel imagined he could identify a drier, brittle aroma of familiar decay.

The green manila folder was tucked firmly under his arm. At the head of the stone steps leading to the courtyard, a black officer was talking to three white squaddies. Vogel nodded as he hurried past the soldiers. They didn't notice.

He had taken the file on a whim. He had found it shortly after lunch when he'd started to sift through a fresh batch of documents. There it lurked, smothered under scores of other secret police reports: a faded lime green file, his name inscribed in oversized red capitals on the front.

Vogel had been astonished. He had not known what to do. At first he wondered if he should hand over this report for another archivist to evaluate and categorize. Instead, he put the dossier aside and waited for a moment, sometime later, when he might feel composed enough to study the contents of his own secret records. He had busied himself with other files.

Examining and classifying documents gave Vogel a sense of serenity, an alluring promise of order and control. Hours of stubborn routine and the application of his fussy, professional detachment gradually calmed him. As he rose to close up his office, Vogel had decided to leave his own file for the next morning. It was only as he was about to duck through the low doorway that, impulsively, he had scooped up the scruffy green file.

In the main courtyard a tour group was being shepherded towards the exit. It was past closing time and they were dawdling. The flustered guide was attempting to hurry them along without jeopardizing her tip. An older man was talking loudly and sounded drunk. His shirt was tied round his waist, his pasty, overhanging stomach emphasizing the raw flush of his knotty, sunburned face.

Vogel strode across the grass, scorched flaxen by heat and drought. His feet were sweating, mouth dry. He hadn't experienced such a ferment of anxiety and exhilaration in, oh, perhaps sixteen or seventeen years. Guiltily, he caught the eye of the tour guide. She was a large woman with a khaki skirt and flat shoes. She shrugged, as if they were complicit in this rear-guard action against disobliging aliens.

"*Mas'ambeni*, my people," she called out, clapping her hands. "Please! Otherwise you must be locked in the Castle for the night."

In the past, on clandestine commissions, he had always dreaded the possibility of challenge. It was his weakness: an uncontrolled eruption of anger when confronted by authority. Yet there was no reason museum wardens should question him - or even the soldiers on guard at the Castle entrance. As a white man, he still retained a certain immunity. Also, they probably would not know it was unlawful for him to remove documents from his office.

Vogel shifted the green folder to his left side and hugged it tighter against his chest, hoping this would make it less noticeable. He wore tan, sun-blanched linen slacks and a sky blue T-shirt, with the name of a famous Italian football club stenciled on the front. He doubtless looked like a tourist. Even so, as he passed through the shaded stone arch, the soldier on guard at the Castle gateway saluted stylishly.

"Evening, sir," he grinned. "Enjoy it, Dr. Vogel."

Once outside the bulky stone ramparts, Vogel was assaulted by the enraged bellow of evening traffic. Taxis on Strand Street hooted aggressively. Drivers, one hand on the wheel, leaned far out of already packed vans to proclaim their distant destinations.

Vogel experienced a sudden, illogical, flush of adrenaline. He set

2

off at a fast pace, diagonally across the Grand Parade. Most of the cars parked there during the day had gone and the hawkers and stall-owners were packing up. Three children sniffing glue at the base of the statue of Edward VII encircled him, hands out, clamouring for small change. He pushed through them brusquely.

The colonnaded façade of City Hall was in shadow. This ornate Victorian imitation of Renaissance grandeur had always represented to Vogel the essence of colonial decorum - even the stone shipped from Britain - as well as proclaiming itself the custodian of stern civic virtues. But it was too late for him to take the file back now. The Castle gates would be locked. He hurried on.

He was astonished by the recklessness, his audacity. It was so uncharacteristic. He was a martinet for observing procedures and regulations. That was what made Vogel outstanding at his job. Taking short-cuts or trifling with convention was fatal for the regulation of trustworthy archives: one deviation from the scheme could introduce a muddle that could spread throughout the system.

As he approached the far corner of the Parade, where the last stall-holders displayed gaudy plastic goods and cheaper clothes, the homeward-bound crowd crushed against him. There would be pick-pockets. He clasped the file firmly with both hands.

This personal deviation from explicit regulations rapidly began to unsettle Vogel. He felt fretful, exposed. He glanced behind to see if anyone had followed him. It was an old habit. This also immediately made him feel furtive, as if admitting to his own guilt. Even in the past - when evading the petty legal dictates of a tyrannical regime had practically been a point of honour for most of his friends - it had been hard for him to break the law.

Vogel liked rules. Minor traffic infractions bothered him excessively. He liked precision. Regulations allowed you to establish where you stood, exactly, as well as providing clear and consistent guidelines for further exploration. Meticulous cataloguing of the apparently haphazard allowed Vogel to feel that he could make sense of an unruly world. The capricious removal of his file from the Castle threatened to subvert this disciplined universe.

The pedestrian indicator at the corner of Darling and Plein was red but the homeward-bound throng pressed across the street. Vogel waited. As the light changed, cars surged ahead, hooting, disregarding their own red traffic sign. Vogel hovered indecisively.

Normally he continued past the old Post Office, then right for the flower market. That was his routine. For over twenty years, at least two or three times every week, he had bought flowers there for Marda. Now, anxious to get home quickly, Vogel turned left. He dashed across Darling and hurried south along the narrower, quieter Plein Street.

Under a once imposing arcade, worn-out shops were locked with grilled gates and security bars. He passed a barricaded halaal take-away. This had none of the expansive colonial elegance of his regular route home. He caught the sour reek of urine. Outside the 'Classic & Modern Dance Emporium' waited two bow-tied young black men. One wore a white straw boater. Vogel clutched the file tighter and glanced away, aware the youths were examining him.

Ahead, evening sunlight slanted eastward across Spin Street. As Vogel neared the intersection, he saw his path was obstructed by a ragged assembly. Twenty or so men waved placards. They had formed a circle round a building site. The group was yelling slogans. They sounded angry. Usually, from custom and sympathy, Vogel lingered at any demonstration. Now he felt apprehensive.

"Leave the bones," he heard indistinctly. "Leave the bones!"

A tall, very dark African man with tribal scarification and white robes stepped into his path. Vogel tried to move round him but found his way blocked.

The vendor beamed. "Watch, sunglasses? Best after-shave …"

"Fuck off," shouted Vogel, startled by his own fury.

"No problem." The man touched his arm gently. "It's stress, Baba. But, hey, I got some best quality pills, man, very nice. Big discount."

The archivist broke into a run. Behind him he heard a shout.

"See a doctor, sir, please …"

Vogel forced himself to slow to a brisk stride.

Six minutes later he stood before his front door, breathless. The slender street was deserted; the silent terraced houses familiar and orderly. Vogel laughed out loud at the absurdity of his fear.

It was the result of cataloguing that freshly unearthed batch of files, he thought; living all day among dismal, crudely specific accounts of police surveillance. Yet Vogel had only to glance down his street to see how much had altered. Once this had been a slum. Now he was sandwiched between an advertising agency and a modish interior decorator. When younger, far more prosperous neighbors had begun restoring rusted wrought-iron balconies and redecorated in jazzy, exuberant pastels - to match the confident, changing times - Vogel had joined in. It was the first time in fifty years his house had been painted. Vogel's home, where he had been born, was now sienna red with a mango yellow door.

Even the street name had been changed. Before, in honour of an early British Governor, it had been "Yonge Street". Then two months ago, without warning, it became Sabata Dalindyebo Way.

Once inside, Vogel habitually placed flowers on the oak sideboard beside a framed photograph of Marda. This evening he went straight to the kitchen. Scarlet bougainvillea blossom lay sprinkled over white marble tiles. The petals, blown through the grilled gate protecting an enclosed courtyard, crunched underfoot as Vogel took a beer from the fridge.

Then, green file still tucked firmly underarm, Vogel climbed the stairs to his balcony. The smoldering sun hung low over Signal Hill. Vogel noticed a plume of smoke rising languidly from the side of Table Mountain, not very far from the cable car station.

He sat in his bamboo rocking-chair, the green file on his lap. By habit Vogel removed his rimless glasses and wiped them on his shirt. Glasses restored, he checked again; yes, his personal dossier. His name had been scrawled in capitals on the front cover with a red felt-tipped pen, while underneath, printed by a formal black stamp, was a case number: CCT10/36.

A luxuriant, guilty thought came to him. He had put off examining his file at work, in the Castle, because he had wanted to enjoy the experience. It was true; he had procrastinated in order to enhance his anticipation.

Here, within this frayed manila folder, was official evidence: the definitive authentication of his clandestine life. Vogel sat staring at the mountain. As dark fell he saw blistering, livid flames. The fire, seemingly harmless by daylight, swelled purple with intensity and violence. He thought of early settlers in Cape Town, haunted by the persistent fear of arson or an uprising, anxiously watching nighttime fires on Table Mountain lit by runaway slaves.

As a light wind veered northward, Vogel imagined he could hear the crackle of flames. He thought of furnaces, barely a decade ago, burning day and night all over the country as officers of the old regime shovelled dossiers, documents, records and reports as fast as they could into the flames. State incinerators could not take the gargantuan weight of all the security files to be destroyed, so iron and steel factories were also employed to incinerate the evidence.

Such conflagrations tormented Vogel: a reckless, almost demonic immolation - an inferno annihilating stories, testimonies, what flimsy confirmation existed of our lives, and he watched late into the night as the fire raged unchecked on the mountainside, still clutching his own lime green file, unopened.

Two

ALL RECORDS, particularly official ones, and most especially security police reports, Vogel had assured the Deputy Minister, should be read like a work of fiction. Even dates, names and places could never be accepted without cross-examination.

"Files," he said, "have a life of their own."

Vogel had been astonished to be telephoned at home by the Deputy Minister. That was five weeks ago. They hadn't spoken or seen each other in over a decade. Minister D.K. Biyela greeted him genially. For a pleasing while they reminisced about youthful, revolutionary times and Vogel, to his surprise, felt flattered. The Minister's tone was light, almost playful. Then just as Vogel was laughing, Minister Biyela became quieter, confiding.

"You can help me, old friend," he murmured. "Help us, actually."

Secret security documents had been seized from the home of a retired general. The general, implied the Deputy Minister, had retained these state records of the old regime for blackmail purposes - possibly to protect himself and other high officers from prosecution. This suggested there would be valuable historic information among the files, remarked Minister Biyela, but also that a number of them were certain to be shockingly, even provocatively, sensitive. Public figures, for example, even Cabinet Ministers, might be revealed as past informers.

"Obviously," added the Deputy Minister casually, "one can't believe everything one reads."

"Of course, D.K., files are capricious. They've minds of their own."

Only Vogel, implied Biyela, could be trusted with such contentious material. In fact, he announced, an indefinite leave of absence had already been arranged from his work at the State Archives in Roeland Street.

"Do I have a choice?" grumbled Vogel, disguising his delight.

The Deputy Minister explained that the files had been secured. They had been stored in a room at the Castle. Only Vogel would have a key. As the Castle was controlled by the military, no one would know what he was doing; nor was he to discuss this with anyone.

"Military law, naturally," cautioned Minister Biyela, "applies."

"Naturally," replied Vogel dryly. "Bit like old times, eh?"

"So Vogel," concluded the Deputy Minister jovially, "don't believe everything you read!"

Vogel chuckled. "Files," the archivist repeated, "have a life of their own."

It was an article of faith. Vogel, as a result, had not found his own file entirely by chance. He had searched for it.

Three days previously he had been examining the security branch dossier on a flamboyant trade unionist. Vogel had never met this man, so he was shaken to discover a flippant remark he'd once made repeated in the file as fact. Vogel's coarse joke about the unionist's reputed partiality for pale, seditious girls and outsized Havana cigars - based purely on hearsay - had been recorded as verified truth. For all Vogel knew, the gossip could have been originated by the security police themselves to discredit one of the most popular leaders of the internal insurrection. The man was now a glamorous retail and property tycoon. Yet here, for posterity, Vogel's careless jest had been solemnly recorded by an anonymous security agent as a credible psychological profile and character assessment.

Vogel remembered making this joke. It had been twenty-seven years before at a secretive weekend party on a farm near Tulbagh. The remark, however, was attributed to the poetess Grethe Cilliers. The official report stated - slyly implying Grethe had intimate background knowledge - that she'd made the claim at a clandestine political meeting in central Cape Town. Perhaps she had repeated his joke; Grethe, after all, had been Vogel's lover.

There had been a cross-referenced number for Grethe Cilliers' dossier. He began an orderly search. Shifting hundreds of documents from one stack to another exhausted him. Chalky dust drizzled over everything. Vogel had almost sifted through the entire stockpile, with no sign of Grethe's file, when he had discovered his own dossier.

The following day that green folder remained at his home, concealed among pants and socks in a locked drawer, still unread, while Vogel resumed work at the Castle. It was now apparent to the archivist that this disorderly collection of files was entirely arbitrary, as if grabbed at random and spirited away in a rush. There were career records of security policemen alongside surveillance reports and detailed profiles of suspected subversives.

It wasn't until mid-afternoon when he heard the husky moan of a city returning home, a filtered hum of traffic and honking taxis, that Vogel recalled that this was Friday. Cape Town wrapped up early on weekends.

Vogel, not wishing to draw attention to himself, locked his office and sauntered down to the courtyard. A squad of camouflaged soldiers drilled under the ramparts, boots snapping on cobbles. Clusters of tourists dawdled on the yellowing grass, evidently more interested in soaking up sunshine than visiting the antique Dutch interiors. Vogel heard French, German, a variety of English accents, Russian and Greek. He felt relaxed, amused. He was jostled by a boisterous group of Spaniards as he exited through the Castle gateway. Out in the bay, a tug whooped.

A skinny, crinkled man in a white jalabiyya tossed pizza to bickering seagulls in the moat. Crossing the Grand Parade, Vogel savoured the glow of sun on his face. At the corner of Darling and Plein, he continued on his normal route, following the crowd past the old Post Office and turned right to the flower market. He'd known some of the older flower vendors for nearly thirty years. As on most Fridays for at least the last four or five months, he bought from the same diminutive cinnamon-soft woman in a purple scarf, selecting an abundant bouquet of orange Tiger Lilies.

The motion of following his regular route home revived Vogel's natural buoyancy. Even the illuminations across Adderley Street, still left over after Christmas - ranks of Caucasian angels and disorientated Wise Men, blanched from a summer of merciless sun - delighted him.

9

Waiting to cross the street outside the stern *Groote Kerk*, opposite the Slave Lodge, he heard, not far eastward, an invisible crowd chant:

"Let the bones sleep, let the bones sleep ..."

As soon as Vogel entered the oak-lined cool of Government Avenue, the broiling clamour of the evening city softened. This was the path to and from work that he'd followed all his adult life: past Parliament, along the shaded pedestrian boulevard and through the heart of the seventeenth century Company Gardens. Hurrying, he could be home in less than ten minutes. Instead Vogel dawdled, relishing the dappled light and hesitant giggles from couples on park benches.

Twenty-five minutes later he reached Sabata Dalindyebo Way.

When he was growing up this had been a poor working-class area, the terraced houses overcrowded and shabby. The neighbourhood had also been racially mixed, until mercilessly purged to create an all white enclave when Vogel was still in his early twenties. Gradually abandoned workshops had been transformed into elegant condominiums. Now there were cafés and tavernas. It lifted the archivist's spirits to see the brash colours in his street - avocado green, succulent peach, his own mango yellow door. To Vogel, this gaudy self-assurance represented clear evidence of his own tortuous journey: that he had moved with the times, without ever having actually moved at all.

Vogel became aware of the tinny clatter of a helicopter, perhaps two, from the direction of Table Mountain. Inside, his living room was dark, curtains drawn. He laid the lilies beside the photograph of Marda. His shoes crunched on bougainvillea petals. Vogel hurried upstairs, onto the balcony.

A fog of brown smoke drifted towards him. The haze was so dense he couldn't see the flames. A lone helicopter swooped, aiming straight at the mountainside, with an ungainly plastic water container dangling underneath. The helicopter vanished into the thick smoke for several heart-constricting seconds; then it skimmed up almost vertically away from the stony cliff-face, empty water container swinging wildly, before curling back towards the bay.

All day, as Vogel had worked systematically through other police files at the Castle, he'd experienced a rising sense of exhilaration at the thought of examining his own record. Now, however, the archivist continued to delay the examination of his dossier. Vogel remembered how as a child, while his older brother Michael rushed to rip open presents at Christmas, he had preferred instead to prolong the suspense, postponing the moment of revelation until his mother and Michael had absolutely insisted.

A skeleton outline of the most exhilarating years of his life - what else? - must be concealed within that bland lime green folder. The full narrative probably only amounted to dry lists in curt bureaucratic idioms: places, dates, names, suspicions. Yet such an inventory would sketch a rough contour of his clandestine life. This thought filled him with pride and anticipation.

Vogel retrieved his file and returned to the balcony. A meek breeze fanned tendrils of smoke westward, browning the setting sun. He sat with the pale green folder on his lap. The helicopter shimmied back into view, followed by another. Both trailed spumes of sea water, and in synchronized runs they dived towards the invisible blaze.

When he had first stumbled across that green folder he had been furious. He had experienced a familiar eruption of rage. His comrades used to call it, 'going off like a fire-cracker.' All recognized this as Vogel's weakness. That was why he was given backroom, monotonous tasks like encoding secret messages. Vogel assumed such flare-ups were incited by a loathing of injustice and that those embers had long subsided. Yet finding his own police record had re-ignited his indignation at the idea of cops snooping about in the detritus of his life with tape-recorders and binoculars.

Of course, he couldn't predict what would be in the dossier. Files, as he'd told Deputy Minister D.K. Biyela, seemed to have a life of their own. Nevertheless, after his initial resentment, even dread, Vogel had begun to delight in the knowledge that he had, after all, been assigned his very own individual secret police file. Here, at last, was official confirmation: written proof of a certain heroic stature.

Vogel had always been a background person. Few today knew anything of his past. He imagined, for example, that his younger neighbours simply saw a slender, still fine-looking man in his fifties, who had probably sleep-walked his way through those years of tyranny by keeping his head down in a tedious job. Would they now be impressed by the evidence of a life of pervasive menace, and the risks he'd taken; that unrelenting, chronic suspense? It was gratifying to imagine, should the contents of his file be made public, that colleagues at least might look upon him with new respect.

And still Vogel put off the pleasure of reading this forgotten story.

Three

ON Saturday afternoon, opening the lime green folder with his name blazoned in capitals on the cover, Vogel discovered that it contained seven red lined, foolscap pages, with some sections typed, others handwritten. Each entry was signed and dated. Though a dozen or more agents had contributed to his file, there was a uniform, impersonal style. This added to the overall impression that it was a trustworthy, strictly factual document.

That morning he had worked at the Castle. It was a way of keeping his rising excitement under control. As he'd left at noon, the soldier at the gateway smiled. "Watching the big match this afternoon, sir?"

"You should search me," suggested Vogel recklessly. "I could be taking government stuff home, you know."

The guard laughed, "Not you, Dr. Vogel," and saluted. "*Ube nemini emnandi.*"

"I'll do my best," replied the archivist, adding cheerily. "You have a good day, too, my friend."

The city was quiet and hot. Vogel had dawdled on his way home, prolonging the suspense. He wanted to savor the contemplation of that moment when he would finally open the green folder. He wanted to be calm, fully prepared to relish the occasion. Friends, events and excitements that he had not evoked in a long while surfaced. It was like watching a silent film. Arbitrary images appeared to him - unexpectedly, delightfully - in a new and daring light. At the flower market he'd bought another two garlands of lilies, a double extravagance always reserved for the weekend. This offering he laid reverently by the photo of Marda; an avowal that she, too, shared his anticipation of the approaching, pleasurably-deferred sacramental moment.

Bougainvillea petals, blown through the house by the previous day's wind, lay limply on the kitchen tiles. The petals had dried and they crackled underfoot as Vogel prepared himself a large sandwich.

He rescued the green folder from its hiding place among pants and socks. Entering his study, by habit, he had locked the door behind him.

As always when about to tackle a new document, the archivist took off his glasses, wiped them; then rapidly skimmed the contents to gain an overall impression. This initial scan, despite days of tension and expectation, seemed at first as humdrum as any other workaday professional appraisal. There was no expected illumination, no shriving revelation.

The archivist was also bewildered by his chilly, totally unexpected detachment. It was as though he were reading about someone he'd never met.

Vogel felt dazed, somehow deflated … even, heartlessly, let down.

A landward breeze sprung up, insinuating and sticky. The temperature kept rising. Vogel felt prickles of sweat on his chest and wondered if he should take a shower. Perhaps that would rouse him out of this curious torpor; this unexpected, tumbling discouragement.

A lone petal, gusted upstairs, lay on the carpet; scarlet faded to russet.

With only one half-shuttered window overlooking the courtyard, his study grew quite dark. He switched on his desk lamp and began to read the first page again more attentively. There were dates of various meetings he'd attended, lists of names of those who had also been present, and a précis of what had been said, by whom.

Mostly these accounts consisted of plain, entirely deadpan facts. He remembered the majority of those occasions; indeed, most had been public demonstrations, details of which could have been gleaned from newspapers. With other entries he had to think for a while before a familiar name or reference reminded him of the event. Some he simply could not recall.

The first page was almost exclusively a list of early protest meetings, often broken up by the police. Vogel may or may not have been present. There had been so many such demonstrations he could not recollect them all. It was dull, unexciting. There was nothing confidential or personal; no hint of his secret life, covert activities, not a trace of heroism.

Vogel experienced a mounting simmer of resentment. He began to feel affronted. He deserved more than this, a paltry register of attendance at public events ... indexed as a mere bit player in the crowd. The archivist now recognized the source of that abrupt sensation of deflation and consequent, enveloping lassitude. He had simply not been given his due.

He should not, he knew, have been surprised. This duplicated the pattern of so many hundreds of similar documents that he had studied: lackluster, derivative and repetitive. Vogel, however, was unable to stifle a rising bile of indignation. If another archivist had examined this dossier, his true role would not be apparent at all. He felt cheated.

"Idle bastards," he muttered aloud.

He had been underestimated, underrated. Undervalued.

It was a professional affront, too. Vogel felt this strongly. A major enjoyment of his work was to measure himself against a gifted antagonist; an agent who honoured the basic detective work - the footslog and lurking, sleuthing and surveillance, but who also possessed a shrewd understanding of his quarry and their aims.

"Worthless," he said, irritably. "Sloppy work, guys."

On the third page he lingered over the half dozen or so paragraphs which mentioned Grethe Cilliers. At first glance these had revealed little beyond dates, timing and places where they had been spotted together, and as several of these entries were handwritten they had been difficult to decipher. But as he examined these sections in more detail, Vogel began to enjoy himself a little more. He deduced from the sparse detail in these accounts that it was Grethe who had been followed to the assignations. Here, too, was a reference code, CCT704, recorded in brackets after her name.

It was clear - at least from this file - that the security police had no idea Grethe and he had been compiling encrypted messages, some to be smuggled abroad, others transmitted to distant parts of the country. This is where comparison with Grethe's missing dossier would help complete the puzzle. It was entirely possible it might contain more informed observations; that some clerk had been indolent in copying details into his file, for instance, or that the agent in charge of her case had deliberately withheld information from colleagues, either from professional habit or in order to grab all the glory of exposure and arrest for himself.

Vogel cheered up. He and Grethe had operated on the assumption that she was the more likely to be under observation, and here was evidence that they had apparently succeeded in outwitting the opposition. Of the frequent occasions he and Grethe met, the police had only managed to track fourteen. Vogel had always relished the intricate stratagems of evasion for their meetings. Assignations with Grethe were cloaked in mystery and danger.

He also noted, with added satisfaction, that their pursuers had no proof that he and Grethe had ever been lovers. Specifics were scanty. One report was reduced to conjecture, remarking that while Vogel remained unmarried, young Grethe, though fleetingly wedded, had recently separated.

It concluded, "Motive for rendezvous … sex?"

He was amused to observe this brief entry relied, for corroboration, on adducing Grethe's magnetism, her feral allure and lustrous ginger hair. If Vogel had been analyzing the file of someone unknown to him he would have taken this as the unreliable, resentful projection of a bored foot soldier. The very next entry, the last on Grethe, merely stated: "Sex? Of course!"

Now that he was paying closer attention, Vogel noted that subsequent entries on the next page, though still meager, were more specific. They no longer referred to public events, but concentrated on clandestine gatherings. He had not detected this on his first, rapid reading. The archivist felt a bristle of expectancy, as always when he discerned a faint shift. At this point, it would seem, he was under closer observation himself. Vogel was no longer an object of attention merely because Grethe led there. He was the hunted.

There was a reference to a meeting on the farm near Tulbagh, but no mention of that crude joke he'd made about the trade unionist which had transferred itself to another file and been attributed instead to Grethe. Vogel experienced a familiar rush of anticipation. This is where his own labour of detection would normally commence: tracking down alternative sources for either verification or perhaps dismissal after cross-reference to other files.

With a random set of records, however, this was not possible. In the case of his own file, it was distressing. He was the best witness. Yet he found much that he couldn't remember.

"Tuesday, March 17th, assembly at home of Jonathan Kavanagh," read one entry. "6 - 8 p.m. Present: Edwin Sarkissian, Sivuyile wakwa Gqabe, Marc Hendricks, Macaulay Vogel, Leonard Barr."

Vogel had no memory whatsoever of such a meeting. There was no other data, suggesting a cop may well have been lurking outside. He vaguely knew of a Jonathan Kavanagh. He had been - still was - an engineer, and as far as Vogel was aware had never been active in underground politics. He found it odd that no address was cited. Just some pitiful informer building up a case or justifying expenses - or had Vogel simply forgotten?

There were other incidents of which he had no recall, links with people he'd never heard of ... or, at least, of whom he had no recollection. There was even one clandestine summit, in Paarl, which he would be prepared to swear, on oath, that he had not attended.

This was disquieting. Vogel would normally balance the veracity of a written contemporary statement against the fallibility of a memory many years later. As a professional, the archivist recognized that he should also, in truth, examine his own dependability.

Page five concluded with a decisive episode that Vogel did remember, vividly. "December 24th, 12 p.m., private conference: Leonard Barr and Macaulay Vogel. Venue: Vogel's house, Yonge Street, Gardens. Time: one hour. Topic: planning and liaison for unlawful general strike in New Year."

Vogel laughed aloud. That was not his role, at all.

"Fooled you," he crowed.

Lenny Barr had indeed come to his home, by prior arrangement, at midnight on Christmas Eve. They'd worked for an hour, feverishly. Lenny trusted him, alone, to encode a decisive message. Vogel asked no questions. He had proved his worth. His discretion was acknowledged. That was the moment Vogel had been - he remembered this with pride - inducted at last into the inner sanctum.

"Way, way off," he chuckled contemptuously. "Not impressed, guys."

Vogel was torn between delight that he'd managed, at least until this point, to conceal his true task - and disappointment that his real significance remained obscure.

When he turned to the sixth page, however, Vogel realized how much he had in fact overlooked by skimming through on his first reading. There were additional, more detailed descriptions of cloak-and-dagger meetings, but alongside bland inventories of those present the archivist now saw there were also increasingly personal notes on his character and behaviour. To begin with he thought nothing of this new development. Then the first report on the final page stated, "Macaulay Vogel left meeting with Sarah (surname unknown)." Another noted, "Vogel departed with Yolande Adams." A third: "Vogel with Natasha Steyn (nee Caplan), leave early, in Steyn's car."

In another paragraph he was jolted by the stark, scribbled phrase, "Vogel drunk."

Names he barely remembered rapidly multiplied, all linked suggestively to him: "Macaulay Vogel & Libby Jacobs" ... "Vogel with Jana Ferreira" ... "Vogel + Mercia Ellis."

This was followed by a terse statement: "Vogel drunk, again."

Vogel was astonished. What had the cops been trying to prove with this tosh? He had come across a couple of references to Marda. But these only recorded her attendance at a meeting. There was no hint that Marda had any connection with him. Vogel was irritated. It was one thing for the cops to miss his affair with Grethe, but he felt oddly troubled, even affronted, that there was no recognition here of his subsequent, profound union with Marda.

"Philistines," he grumbled, hurt. "And what about love?"

There was something deeply unsettling to Vogel in the fact that Marda was denied in the written record. Worse, that his love, the one that had dominated his life ever since, should be trivialized by being submerged by all those other women, most of whom Vogel barely remembered.

He repeated incredulously, "Gina Drummond? Unity de Beer? Dulcie Jordaan?"

Now that at last he saw these names, they leapt out at him everywhere.

Some had a file reference number, others didn't, with no apparent logic.

In these pithy, throwaway remarks a clear portrait was building up relentlessly. There was nothing about his studious habits, his love of walking or hikes on the mountain. There was nothing in these reports that Vogel recognized and he felt a throb of disgust.

Towards the bottom of the page he found two further comments, even bolder, written in two different handwritings, probably added later by more senior agents after reading the typed reports. One said, "Womaniser." The other: "Alcohol ... drunkard?"

This was a travesty. Vogel felt a spreading, familiar prickle of bitterness and escalating fury.

"Lies," he snapped. "All bloody lies."

How could he possibly sustain a professional objectivity? This was fiction. Worse, it was like reading his own obituary. Facts and declarations about one's very life, even the most intimate aspects, engraved in back and white ... with each aspect misconstrued or crudely traduced, to be ogled over by strangers. Worst of all, there was nothing he could do.

"Damn you," he hissed. "Goddam hoodlums."

In the final paragraph, tucked away in a tedious report among an extended inventory of names and topics of conversation at a party attended by several well-known dissidents - so buried that he'd missed this on his initial reading - the archivist found a reference to the wife of a friend, Julius Horak. The couple, Vogel recalled, had been at that party. Julius, his wife and two small children had died shortly afterwards in a car accident.

A postscript declared, "M. Vogel long affair Isobel Horak. Married women, his weakness?"

"Not true," he gasped.

There followed, in brackets, a serial number, with the terse addendum: "For Vogel, other lovers, see personal file."

"You swine," he whispered.

Even now, all these years later, his tormentors were keeping secrets from him and from each other. Hastily, he pushed the green folder into his desk drawer and unlocked the study door. Vogel could smell the smoke even before he walked out onto the balcony.

The wind had revived and changed direction. In the dark, he saw the cinders on the scorched mountainside had been fanned again. Several fierce fires flamed brightly.

Who was this individual depicted in his file?

Words had fallen cruelly, randomly, lying forever in his dossier with no regard for truth or memory. As he watched vivid flames light up the night mountain, he thought of the state incinerators incessantly cremating secret documents. Vogel felt silky caresses slither against his face, like blossom, irritating his eyes. On the floor, by the glow of a street lamp, mixed with a scattering of sun-bleached bougainvillea petals he saw a layer of grey ash.

He felt a rage he had not experienced in a decade. His eyes misted.

"No," Vogel whispered. "That's not me ..."

Then, loudly: "Bastards!"

Four

"FILES" - his own words mock him - "have a life of their own."

Vogel does not recognise this person depicted in his own dossier.

As an archivist, Vogel has developed the custom of reading files as if they were a crime novel. Separate facts have to be shepherded into a coherent unity, then cross-referenced with clues and details from other files, so that a character could come to life. Vogel never takes a statement or testimony at face value. Any dossier is likely to be compromised by an amalgam of bias, small-mindedness or misinterpretation. Informants might be motivated by greed or jealousy. As he is aware from close friends who had suffered, much information was extracted under unbearable isolation or torture. Even among the heroes there is also vanity, avarice, alcohol, debt and infidelity.

Vogel has developed particularly sensitive antennae to detect the self-aggrandizement of policemen. He is acutely aware that most of the agents compiling these reports were intent on furthering their careers, so it was in their interest to exaggerate their prowess of detection and the assumed culpability of the suspect.

Once a police dossier was under way, as in most thrillers or a movie, accounts tended to confirm the character already sketched: observations that contradicted this portrait were suppressed or downplayed while details confirming the overall picture were highlighted. Working out the weaknesses and foibles of those who compiled the report is part of the enjoyment for Vogel, as is sifting authentic mistakes from outright fabrication. Then there are the casual remarks, often from spite or envy, that find their way into someone else's file, instantly assuming - like Vogel's crude joke - the menacing weight of truth.

Yes, files have a life of their own.

Vogel first became aware of this when, after his indecisive arts degree at the University of Cape Town, he had enrolled at the State Archives in Queen Victoria Street. Once qualified as an archivist, he continued as a state employee for another twelve years, a steadfast cover for his subversive activities, before branching out into private and corporate archival work. The problem, however, always remained the same: the fugitive nature of facts. In the end, and triumphantly, after the sclerotic *ancien regime* finally imploded, he had been invited back to the State Archives ... only to find his dilemma greatly intensified. Vogel's new job was to corral into the archives all that had previously been excluded or ignored: in other words, any evidence or material testimony of the lives of indigenous people so disdained by both the colonial and industrialised worlds.

His task was to locate confirmation of those who had not been caught in any written annals, certificates, contracts, wills or public protocols: in fact, the majority, those who had been written out of the record. Yet Vogel sensed that such shards of memory - rock paintings, domestic relics, oral histories - were inherently unwilling to be trapped in official registers, or even indoors.

This feeling of imprisonment was accentuated by the fact that, since he had last worked for that department, the State Archives had been moved right across town from Queen Victoria Street to Cape Town's nineteenth century prison, the Roeland Street goal. Working behind massive grey stone walls, like battlements, with an entrance modeled on a medieval castle portcullis, Vogel suspected more than ever that his job was increasingly like that of a warder or jailor: to incarcerate restless, often unwilling, information.

He is, oh certainly he is convinced: files undoubtedly do have a life of their own. The archivist is all too well aware, for example, that a sliver of information transferred to another file can take on a wholly different slant. It creates a new relationship, an alternative interpretation - especially when studied by another department, or an agent searching for confirmation of guilt. Scraps of information seep out, multiply, flourish and develop an existence of their own. Once nestling in another file, their significance is transformed, capable of shedding a totally contrary light to that revealed in the original file.

If factual, the data is subtly altered, so as to no longer be strictly true. If false, it can be re-adjusted to seem even truer. As in most glittery movies where characters must forever act out their 'character', without really doing the unexpected or improbable, so these errant splinters of information could seem to be consistently real and true, thus doubly damning.

Files "leak", he had informed Deputy Minister D.K. Biyela. They ooze and mingle. They seep unnoticed into one another. Vogel believed this dynamic to be especially treacherous when documents languish in an office or storeroom for a long time, only consulted intermittently when other officials later dip into them in search of different clues.

Such migrations of information, with time, gather a momentum of their own. Vogel has found instances where the movement is circular, returning data eventually to the original file, and thereby - recycled full circle - adding apparently independent corroboration; thus finally delivering the required proof for what had only started out as a suspicion.

The longer the files are left, Vogel has discovered, the truer they seem. The fallible hand that wrote them appears distant, invisible, and the record under inspection takes on the weight of history. As folders gather dust, they decay, they crumble. Like corpses, they infect and corrupt their immediate surroundings, and the past seeps into the present.

Five

LATE on Saturday afternoon he watched the soccer match on television. Vogel found it difficult to concentrate. His eyes remained fixed on the TV screen. His thoughts, however, circled back to what had been in his dossier. He felt shaken, nervous, sullen and disoriented. It was as if he were sedated: the images of himself and past events which had surfaced earlier, like a silent black and white movie, were blurred and jumpy, with no cohesion or logic, jumbled up with throbbing TV colours and distorted by the hullabaloo of the soccer commentary and strident intermission adverts. Originally the discovery of his file had curiously reassured Vogel, as though he were on the verge of locating his place in history: as if, at last, he were about to witness himself, his true self, mirrored in that past. Now it was as if that mirror had been shattered by a brutally gloved hand, and he simply couldn't see himself reflected there anymore.

On Sunday he rose before dawn. He'd fallen asleep on the couch. The TV was still on. He was due to meet Edwin and Rafik at seven-thirty. On the last Sunday of every month, the three of them climbed the mountain. They had performed this ritual for over twenty years. It had begun as a way to escape scrutiny, so they could talk freely or exchange information. There was no longer any need for such stratagems. Even so, they still maintained the discipline. No one else - wife, friend or lover - was allowed to join.

Vogel was the first. He parked beyond the lower cable station. The sun was already broiling. His eyes felt scratchy and tired, as if he were suffering from a hangover. Unable to absorb what he had read yesterday, he still felt dazed and apprehensive, like the jitteriness from a nightmare which lingers on into the next day. Perhaps, he thought, like a hangover this feeling will recede. Rafik announced his arrival moments later, hooting gleefully.

"Hey," yelled Rafik, "you'll need mega sun block today, white boy."

Vogel grinned as they shook hands, "Whatever, comrade - but for some of us, and I'll mention no names, it's high time for an emergency diet."

Rafik had always been naturally plump. He was wearing frayed jeans shorts and a psychedelic silk shirt. Rafik seemed, to Vogel, to be unchanged from when they first met.

Edwin, typically, was five minutes late. As he swung out of his shiny silver-grey Mercedes, he waved. Without a word the three began their ascent. Edwin was always the best equipped: high-tech hiking boots, russet cotton sports shirt and floppy bush hat. His aged military-service rucksack, with water bottles swinging from its leather straps, contained a large thermos of coffee and, prepared by Susan, sandwiches and cake for all.

Edwin was tall, trim and polished. They'd met at university over three decades ago; Vogel diffident and insecure, Edwin Sarkissian unnervingly self-assured. The only difference in the passing years, it seemed to Vogel, was that Edwin's wavy blond hair had turned a billowing chalky white.

The stony path led alongside a ravine. The drought had dried up the small stream. By the time they reached the contour path, Vogel was sweating. They had chosen the Platteklip ascent, a wide gorge followed by the first Europeans to climb Table Mountain. The trail zigzagged steeply and the three friends toiled upward in comfortable silence.

Vogel settled into a mechanical pace with the reassuring crunch of stones underfoot. With the lulling heat and breathless climb, his gloom began to lift. Take a more professional perspective, he told himself, put some detachment between you and your file. In fact, ever since his initial anger had subsided, he'd felt quite disconnected from his own emotions. He tried to concentrate on the steep path, but his thoughts soon looped back to the haphazard stacks of files at the Castle.

It worried him that there was no discernable pattern. Without a consistent order he could not check the reliability of these records, let alone assess any historic value. He wondered if more documents had been unearthed - and whether, to avoid any one person gaining a coherent picture, there might be other archivists with other secret files in other parts of the country, each unaware of the labours of their colleagues.

Why were there no files there on far more prominent members of their local underground network like Sivuyile, Rafik ... or Edwin, who had been arrested and held in solitary confinement? Apart from Vogel's file, there'd only been that one terse mention of Grethe Cilliers, and a reference number for her missing file. They had guessed at the time that Grethe was under observation. She'd been, after all, a young Afrikaans poetess of a certain notoriety. She was also, back then - and Vogel had learned not to discount such factors when trying to ascertain why security police might decide to concentrate on one suspect rather than another - spectacularly good-looking.

He had lost contact with almost all those companions. Two had died, several had moved to Johannesburg, one had emigrated. Most though had simply drifted into other lives: marriages, careers ... in short, ordinary life. The memory of their loyalty, optimism, camaraderie in adversity, was what still endowed Vogel with value and purpose. Just as classifying documents offered him a sense of order in an apparently otherwise muddled universe, so the recollection of those friends, and hardships shared, gave shape to his life.

The prospect that the collection of files at the Castle had been put together merely by chance wrapped Vogel with unease. When work went well he felt as if each word in the archive had slotted into a satisfying pattern. But at other times words seemed to scatter into whimsical configurations with no form or significance. Years ago, when they were composing coded messages to be smuggled abroad, he had joked with Greta that he sometimes dreamed that while the documents were unattended at night legions of imperceptible insects would ferry individual words, letter by letter - or even whole sentences - between files, marching purposefully back and forth under the cover of dark like armies of well-drilled ants, so that by morning all would seem the same but the records themselves would be utterly changed.

As they climbed higher, the gorge grew steeper. They'd been walking for nearly three hours. Behind, with each step, Rafik gasped audibly.

Vogel wondered if he should alert Grethe to the fact that he had found a reference to her security file and that he now even knew her surveillance code number. Did allegiance to a former lover outweigh his current professional obligations? No, he wouldn't tell her. They lived, at last, in a social order they had fought to establish, so breaking the rules was no longer an act of conscience. To publicize or not was now a problem for others: the Deputy Minister, for example. Vogel's continuing contribution to the increase of public well-being was simply to sort, classify and evaluate public records.

The sun was scalding as they clambered the final stretch to the summit. Edwin led the way along the mountain face until he found an outlandishly wind-furrowed, overhanging rock.

"We'll take a five minute break," he groaned as they collapsed in the shade. Edwin passed around a water bottle. "Did you count how many people overtook us ... whole families, teenagers, even kids?"

They gulped the water. Vogel wiped a vapor of sweat from his eyes.

"Ten years ago that would've taken us half the time," admonished Edwin. "Not good, fellas."

"Let's have lunch," suggested Rafik when he had regained breath.

"No, we push on," replied Edwin. "Get a better view."

"The view's fine," said Rafik. "I'm hungry."

"Sandwiches and coffee later." Edwin chuckled, "No kidding, guys, your discipline's totally *slapgat*."

Vogel stared at the city below: beyond, the great ocean lapped over an immaculate blue horizon. He never tired of this panorama. Vogel could make out the granite grey pentagon of the seventeenth century Dutch Castle. He traced his route from work: the tarmac expanse of the Grand Parade, the slim thread of Adderley Street bisecting the city centre, the tranquil emerald green of the Company Gardens. From this height, the narrow compass of his life was apparent, and the contained routine of it filled Vogel with delight.

A haze of pollution hovered to the north-east over the ever spreading shantytowns. Millions of abject hovels engorged across the sandy plains, surrounding the gleaming modern city like a besieging medieval army, entirely cutting Cape Town off from Africa.

Eventually Rafik said: "No one elected Edwin to decide."

"Time's up," announced Edwin, rising. "More water before we go?"

Rafik cleared his throat, resentfully. "I suggest we vote on this."

"Oh c'mmon Rafi, shake a leg, old man. Vogel?"

They rose stiffly and followed in single file as Edwin led them along the high plateau. As they neared the upper cable station, there were more people; couples, families, organised groups.

"Tourists," grumbled Rafik loudly. "Damn locusts."

"Shh," admonished Edwin. "Besides, that's lots more money for you, Rafi."

"Damn tourists," repeated Rafik, louder. "Like flies on a sticky cake."

As they passed the upper cable station, Edwin stooped without breaking his stride to pick up several plastic bags and empty juice cartons. He folded them into his rucksack.

"Right, over there," he pointed. "That's our spot."

"Edwin, there's no damn shade," objected Rafik.

"We've got hats, Rafi. It's the view we're after." They scrambled down to the ledge and settled on the blistering rock. Below, on the saddle descending towards the outskirts of the city, was a desolate sheathe of charred mountainside. The fire had consumed most of the westward slope. After four months of drought, the scrub had blazed aggressively. Flames had jumped the road and appeared almost to have reached - out of sight - the first line of homes. Drifts of smoke still leaked from the blackened gradient. Sporadic embers flickered in the charcoal waste.

"Police say it's arson," remarked Edwin, pouring coffee into the plastic thermos cup. He handed Vogel a sandwich. "Susan says that's just police bullshit. I mean, how can one tell if a bush fire like that is deliberate?"

Edwin tugged the brim of his linen hat lower, crinkling his eyes to focus better. "With a really big wind, though, in the right direction, I guess a forest fire could one day pretty much cook the whole freaking city."

They ate in silence. After a while, Rafik said: "We should've stayed in the shade."

The air floated with a smoky aroma of dead, seared vegetation.

"You hear about the bones in Spin Street?" asked Edwin. "Yeah, a stack of bones were excavated." He laughed. "So now some angry Muslim guys are marching up and down with placards, yelling their heads off and claiming the wicked construction company is desecrating slave remains."

"Even slaves," replied Rafik, "should be allowed to rest in peace."

"No one knows where slaves were buried."

"This is right across from the Slave Lodge."

"Not the point, Rafi. No one has any idea at this stage whether they're slaves or white riff-raff. These fanatics don't want the bones moved at all."

"Ah ... so what you're really worried about, in fact, is that this will stop the development of a five-star super-luxury hotel!"

"Oh please, they won't even permit any scientific analysis. This is superstition ... they're already treating those bloody bones like holy relics."

"Your ancestors have tombstones," pointed out Rafik. "White people have burial sites. They put up plaques, have memorials. But we, it seems, must remain anonymous."

Vogel felt languid and peaceful. Wryly he recalled how at university Sarkissian seemed to embody all those qualities that he then felt he lacked himself: popular, swashbuckling, with an enviably casual assurance about his future. In contrast, when he'd met Rafik, Vogel instantly recognised the familiar signs: hesitancy, an instinct to defer, to seek and accept anonymity. Vogel tried to remember the occasion when he'd first encountered Rafik. He couldn't. Precision from the past, he realised, was gently beginning to fade.

As Vogel contemplated the city before him he could clearly distinguish all those circles of exclusion that had once driven him to violent rebellion: the affluent European city centre, motorways and railways that cordoned off the wretched townships; the great sandy wasteland glinting with shacks as far as the eye could see. Examining this was like having his past laid out before him. Yet now all that seemed distant, much smaller: over.

He became aware that the voices of his companions had grown

more heated. He listened with detached amusement. Once, Vogel reflected, he would have flared up too.

"This is a slave city, but you'd never know it," declared Rafik, his voice taut. "No street names, monuments or statues. It's a city in denial, Edwin - just like you."

Vogel felt lightheaded, pleasantly removed, as if floating. He could now eavesdrop on such fierce arguments and not get angry. Words seem to flutter around him gently. He noticed lower down the blackened slope that stumps of ravaged pine trees were smoldering more intensely, their roots still alight beneath the earth, exhaling plumes of scented smoke.

"Bollocks, this is just a religious rip off," objected Edwin. "In fact, I'm quite shocked you're going along with this, Rafi. Yeah, actually, it's quite reactionary, y'know. I mean, if the bones aren't tested, you could be venerating shipwrecked sailors or white plague victims for all we know."

"You think this is about science, progress?" Rafik asked incredulously.

His face was puffy, hurt. "You just don't understand, you white people. Leave us be, man. Stop telling us what's best for ourselves."

He plucked up a fist-sized rock and heaved it down the charred slope.

"Billy agrees with me," he added defiantly. "That's what Billy thinks, too."

They withdrew into silence: the noonday sun, merciless; the stilled air, moistureless. Cape Town looked exposed and vulnerable.

Words, which only a while ago seemed to flutter gently to the ground like spring blossom, now appeared to be blown aimlessly, scattered without sequence on barren soil, instantly turned black with the blistering heat. Maybe words like freedom, hope and liberty had never meant the same things to Rafik and Edwin; perhaps they had only ever imagined it.

Six

IN the following days Vogel suffered. He was distressed. Then at unexpected moments he was livid again. Bitterness throbbed like a fever. As the week passed, roasting and uncertain, this prickly agitation deepened. He raged. He agonized. He was alternatively indignant, then self-pitying.

The anguish, as ever, was induced by the arbitrary exercise of power.

Vogel could not ease the acidic, corroding ache of resentment. He had been traduced. Who on earth was this person described in his file? There was no recognition of his consequence or worth. Even Marda … expunged from his life, denied! Instead, he had been portrayed as a drinker and a womanizer. Vogel felt defiled. It was the sense of helplessness he loathed. There was no recourse. Once again, even from that firmly displaced past, anonymous officials had reached out to define him and nullify his value.

The injustice scoured his soul. All week he worked agitatedly in his office at the Castle to find that 'personal' dossier referred to so briefly in the report which he still concealed at home. He moved heaps and bundles and mounds of documents back and forth, as he had done the previous week, in the hope that among those grimy files he may have overlooked the vital one.

The disorder was unbearable: in his office, in the files, in his mind. It was so characteristic of the distrustful, furtive mentality of secret policemen that they should maintain two files for the same person, probably at different departments. That was the bilious way they looked upon the world, not only at suspects but also their own colleagues: everyone was treacherous. It was a noxious, caustic attitude which permeated through the archives, leaking from one file to another, drip by drip, corroding all value and decency.

Vogel was sure that if he could only uncover his other file then at least he would have something to evaluate. It had to contain more facts and accurate data. Most certainly there would be greater substance and precision in that dossier; probably there would also be a sound evaluation of his character as well as a truthful acknowledgment of his significance.

Heat rose brutally throughout the week, magnified by a renewed blaze on the mountain. Vogel heard helicopters droning distantly, ineffectually battling the fires. Even the air seemed shriveled, as if flames had sucked out all the oxygen from the city. Buds of ash began to float into his office. The whitewashed walls were discoloured. Slatted glare filtered through green shutters. Outside the ocean light was blinding. Sea gulls, infuriated, circled and shrieked. The archivist rummaged obsessively and sweated.

After three days Vogel realized that he was simply rearranging files, transferring them from one stack to another, doggedly re-ordering the chaos. But still he pressed on. His confined room seethed with dust. At night he returned home, exhausted. Smoke clogged the streets. As the wind skittered and veered, so did the fires on the mountain, shifting direction unexpectedly and spreading with giant leaps, defeating all efforts to contain the inferno.

Leaving work late, Vogel took the quickest route. Each evening the throng on the corner of Spin Street grew larger, undeterred by the coagulating humidity and brown haze.

"Leave the bones," they chanted passionately. "Let the bones sleep."

As Vogel hurried past he noticed the protest seemed better organized. The crowd now formed a blockade, two deep, surrounding the construction site. Obscured by smoke, he could hear someone lead the chant through a megaphone, voice gravelly with smoke and repetition. "Let the bones sleep."

On Thursday evening Mary Xaba called. She and Zechariah had been worried, she said. They had not heard from him. Mary invited him to dinner the next night.

Vogel declined. "Sorry," he explained wearily. "This is a rush job."

Vogel had known and worked with Zechariah long before Zech had been captured and imprisoned for thirteen years. Mary had been his lawyer. Since their marriage, the Xabas always tried to match him up with a woman.

"You sure you're okay, love?" asked Mary.

"Of course," he replied and concluded the conversation rapidly.

Among the archivist's small circle of friends it was often remarked, though not to his face, that Vogel had turned his home into a mausoleum. He seldom invited anyone to his house, preferring to meet in cafés or the Greek taverna in the cobbled square nearby. He seldom drew the curtains in his living room, and so the ground floor had a slightly lugubrious, funereal air. Whenever he had a visitor Vogel put away the framed photograph of Marda. The only people allowed to see it were the Xabas, who openly reproved him for preserving his home - and life, they said - in silhouette.

"Open the curtains," Mary Xaba fussed. "Let sunlight in."

"You mean a woman," riposted Vogel.

It was a rite they observed, as trusted friends, every time they met. Zechariah and Mary watched over Vogel and fed him often, as if he were a lost waif. You've adopted me, the archivist objected in mock alarm. Indeed, as he never saw his brother Michael, they were in effect now his family. He was bound to them by ties not only of protracted affection but mutual beliefs and shared dangers. The Xabas were the only friends with whom he felt able to broach the subject of Marda, and then only in passing, flippantly.

"Draw back the curtains," Mary urged. "Open up your life, love."

"Mac," Zech would add gently, "it's been twenty-five years."

The house in Sabata Dalindyebo Way gave Vogel exactly that sense of order and stability he craved. His lonely, terrified mother had created for their beleaguered family a citadel against a hostile society. It had been their retreat from a fractious universe. When all was in flux and unmanageable, Vogel still felt this home was a sanctuary. That is why he had stayed on, clung to the spot where he'd been born. It offered him reassurance in a muddled and changing world. Vogel did not want to draw back curtains. He didn't want to let more sunlight in, nor did he desire to open up his life.

"Let the bones sleep."

The chant, distorted by megaphone, disconcertingly resurfaced in his mind. Only now did the thought occur to him that the amplified, leading voice sounded improbably familiar, if indistinct.

Heat consumed the closed-up house. Flakes of ash covered everything. The lilies had wilted into a soiled brown tangle. Upstairs, like a malevolent spirit, Vogel sensed the lurking presence of his dossier. He felt enveloped by the past, asphyxiated.

It was the ephemeral mention of Marda in his file that most distressed the archivist. The fact that she had been merely listed as being present at a couple of meetings, with no other information, tormented Vogel. It was as if Marda possessed no further substance or reality. In the archive, for those who had sat in judgment upon them for so long, she was reduced to a token, marginal note, then carelessly dropped, instantly forgotten ... forever.

She had been written out of the story.

There was no mention of how Marda looked: rangy, with restless grey eyes and slim stretched neck, strong nose and that impatient flick of short-cropped, midnight black hair. No one could have missed her in a room full of people. Marda had magnetism, verve. She radiated conviction. How could any wretched informer not have been captivated by her laugh? How could they not have detected, and recorded, her natural fragrance, a scent of lime and honey that Vogel always sensed in any room long after she had departed?

The blank listing of her name robbed Marda of any human lustre, her due. It eliminated her importance. It disregarded her bravery and passion. Above all, for Vogel, the lack of any further detail simply obliterated from the record any association with him. It denied - no, worse - it ignored their love, the most important fact of his life. In the face of such casual annihilation Vogel felt first rage, then overwhelming lassitude and despair.

For the archivist, the fact that his profound dedication for Marda went unobserved, or was deemed so undeserving of mention, undermined the delicate sense of order and meaning he had been able to fashion, again, in his life. That his love appeared too trivial to witness or record revived a sense of futility that Vogel had not experienced since Marda's death.

She had been killed twenty-five years ago. Vogel kept her framed photo in his darkened living-room, but he did not permit himself to dwell on the circumstances of her death. He kept Marda's memory alive by thinking of her as he had loved her in that moment of intensity, with all young love's self-involved assurance that their delight would survive for eternity. After that, he had simply locked the door on his emotions, just as he had since enclosed his home into a lonely memorial. He had deployed his professional detachment and the study of archives to keep the past at a safe, speculative remove. Now his own file had let that past batter back in, unbearably.

Marda had been murdered. At first they naturally assumed she had been assassinated. After leaving a late night meeting she had been found by a street cleaner at 6 a.m. the following morning in a side-street, not far from the Gardens. Marda had been struck wildly, savagely, on the head, eleven times. Eventually, however, even the most suspicious comrades, despite ingrained mistrust of the police, conceded that this had been a brutal, irrational crime - seemingly gratuitous. It was the senselessness of it that, above all, undermined Vogel. If, for example, Marda had been assassinated in the course of their struggle, he might have found a little solace. Had she been 'removed' by the state or 'eliminated' by secret agents, then this unbearable tragedy could have appeared to carry some purpose, a pattern, even a horrible but heroic logic. It could have been understood, placed in a wider, nobler context. But entirely random, utterly pointless?

Files, once his saviour, had suddenly undermined him. Vogel was overwhelmed by a raw sense of worthlessness and self-disgust. Long forgotten or suppressed feelings and memories bubbled up in chaotic sequence. The order and meaning he had laboured so hard to construct from other people's files now seemed to implode from within his own dossier.

He thought he knew who he was; yet in the official record he was depicted as someone else entirely. It was true that when younger he was more exuberant and spontaneous. But a drunken and thoughtless womanizer?

On Friday, at work, asphyxiated by smoke from the molten furnace of the fires, he found it impossible to focus on the folders in front of him. Vogel had an inordinate faith in words when typed or printed, a conviction that words were the foundation of restoring order and significance to an anarchic universe. Now the letters appeared to break apart incoherently, as if scattered by chance: AHD, FXM, V and L, Q and P and C and Z, forming no intelligible sequence, no longer making any sense; instead creating nonsense or anti-sense, even generating new, unintelligible realities of their own.

The blaze raged uncontrolled. In the afternoon, the wind dropped and when Vogel emerged onto the Castle ramparts he felt a soft flutter of ash. A blanket of dry fog had fallen on the hot city. As he crossed the Grand Parade, indistinct figures loomed out of the cinereous vapour, hurrying by. No one talked. He could hear no traffic. There was an uneasy, menacing silence.

Vogel took the short-cut. The side-streets were deserted. It was a monochrome, hovering world. The stillness was unnerving, like the illusory timeless hiatus of an eclipse. As he hurried south toward the invisible mountain, ash and burning cinders began to rain down more heavily.

Bizarrely, he heard a frenzied trill of cicadas.

Sunlight had turned into twilight. Time and nature appeared reversed. Vogel thought of Pompeii. As he gasped for breath, the clogged air burned his throat. Vogel wondered if this was what it would be like to be interred alive; hermetically sealed for the next 1,700 years. Abruptly, disconcertingly, he remembered that not far from those Roman ruins his own brother had spent lonely years of exile in Naples: another city by a bay in the shadow of an overbearing mountain.

The archivist felt he was hurrying home to inevitable calamity.

At the corner of Spin Street he made out the considerable crowd of demonstrators. They, too, were huddled and silent. But as he passed by, almost as if he had been spotted, that same rasping voice, vaguely familiar, followed him huskily through the megaphone:

"Leave the bones … let the bones sleep!"

By the time Vogel reached Sabata Dalindyebo Way scalding cinders were floating down fast. As they fluttered onto the cobles, some still glowed.

Inside, on the ash-strewn carpet, once scarlet petals were roasted black.

Vogel was disoriented. He felt exactly the same sensation about the man who'd just entered his front door as when he had examined his own file.

This was not a person that he recognized.

Seven

SUSAN Sarkissian was already seated at their usual table by the window of the café in Church Square when Vogel arrived, exactly on time. She had been pretending to read the *Cape Times*, with her back to the door. Yet directly Vogel strode in Susan turned eagerly and rose to greet him. As she leaned close, Susan flicked her well-groomed auburn hair, shimmering with health and expensive care, as a younger woman might artlessly attempt to draw attention to her most flattering attribute.

Her grey-blue eyes sparkled with amusement.

"Darling," she murmured, "you're quite the hermit."

Susan held his gaze with a practiced smile, as if greeting a colleague. With a silky tan and girlish covering of freckles, Susan glowed with merely a touch of make-up. Vogel breathed in a scent of sea salt and sunshine. She kissed him on the lips swiftly but firmly. Vogel licked a strawberry flavor of freshly-applied lipstick.

"Well, at least it's cool in here," remarked Vogel politely, for the benefit of anyone who might be observing. The café was already filling up with lunchtime patrons. He sat down, then added, "That's a helluva racket."

From the corner of Spin Street, just out of sight, the unvarying chant from the demonstration surrounding the building site had grown louder as numbers had swelled. Vogel estimated the crowd was twice the size it had been on Friday, with women in shawls and scarves now joining the men who had taken to marching in a circle around the stalled bulldozers.

"If this heat-wave goes on much longer," he said, "we'll all go crazy."

Susan nodded briskly and lowered her voice again. "Thank you, darling, I think we've done quite enough of the formal bit, don't you?"

Out of the huge picture window of the café, overlooking Church Square, Vogel had a clear view of the *Groote Kerk* and the double-story bulk of the Slave Lodge, with its white walls and green shutters. The air was luminous, a bright amber. Over the weekend a south-east wind had stolen up, dispersing the pall of smoke that had choked the city. In the following days most of the fires had been extinguished, leaving much of the mountainside charred and smouldering. The heat, however, had continued to rise.

Vogel appraised Susan cautiously. "You're looking very ..."

"Very?"

"You know."

"Oh, such sweet talk!"

"I mean, lovely. As always." Vogel hesitated. "Very ... composed."

Susan wore a fashionably tailored, lily-white linen trouser suit. A tall woman, she carried herself with vigorous grace and assurance. Vogel was aware that even though she had just celebrated her fifty-first birthday several men walking by on the pavement outside the café had turned to look at her.

Susan pretended to study the menu. "You've been very elusive," she said softly. "Is anything the matter?"

Vogel had resumed work at the Castle on Monday. But unable to concentrate, on Wednesday morning he had called Susan at her work and told her that he needed to see her urgently.

"I've been going crazy," she grinned. "I thought you'd never phone!"

Vogel picked up the *Cape Times*. There was a picture of a mangled, blackened crane. A small home-made bomb had exploded overnight in the docks. There'd been no explanation for the bomb; no trace of a motive.

"There," he said. "This heat really is driving people crazy."

The waitress, a young Muslim girl in smock and scarf, took their lunch order, and as soon as she had departed Vogel leaned forward.

"Susan," he said softly. "There's something I need to ask you."

42

"Oh, listen to that racket! You'll just have to speak louder, darling. Honestly, what do these people want anyway? I mean, they're all yelling so much one can hardly hear what they're saying." She beamed at him again, trustingly, and Vogel noticed the fine mesh of tiny lines that crinkled around her eyes and broad mouth, and he felt a twinge of tenderness at this rare sign of disorder in Susan's otherwise scrupulously primed appearance. "Besides, I bet most of them don't have a clue what the hullabaloo is really all about."

"It's about the bones," replied Vogel. "They don't want them to be moved from the building site. There are so many bones they say it must have been a mass burial site - and that those are actually the remains of slaves."

Susan inclined her head slightly, eyes steadfastly on Vogel, to show him that she was listening attentively. He knew this was a mannerism, one Susan had been taught to deploy with men; nonetheless he was childishly gratified every time, still in thrall to such intense focus, with its implication that she found his every word intriguing.

"Church Square began as a graveyard," Vogel continued, gesturing towards the *Groote Kerk*. "It was the first cemetery in Cape Town. Most of the early European citizens would've been buried here. Even this café, in the eighteen century, might've been part of the first official burial ground - for white people. There was also a watchman to chase dogs away."

He paused: "But no one knows where most slaves were buried."

"All the same," replied Susan firmly, "there's no proof that these bones are slave remains. Edwin says this is just emotive grandstanding. I mean, they could be skeletons of people who died long ago in a smallpox epidemic or something. Asian, black, white, whatever - we don't know. Edwin thinks something else is going on. Edwin says it's all quite sinister."

Vogel was amused to think of Susan, head tilted charmingly to one side, listening to Edwin with the same flattering seriousness. He wondered, as he did every time he climbed Table Mountain with Edwin, whether her husband knew. On the whole, he thought he probably did. It didn't worry Vogel. He felt no guilt. For nearly six years he and Susan had met a couple of times a month. It was a convenient, almost efficient, arrangement. Vogel never asked Susan about Edwin. He knew she was wholly dedicated to her husband, and appreciated that any endearments or professions of intensity were for her own private enchantment and not to be taken seriously. They both understood this.

"Edwin says that as we fought against one form of bigotry, so now we mustn't give in to another, just because they're ... well, you know." Susan touched his arm. "Edwin feels that very strongly. He says they're religious extremists, just playing on our sense of guilt. What do you think, darling?"

"Slaves didn't have formal cemeteries," said Vogel. "They were just dumped outside white graveyards or in waste ground, where packs of dogs scavenged on the corpses. That's why, you see, in Church Square they employed a watchman to keep the dogs away from the white cemetery."

"You too," murmured Susan triumphantly. "Like Edwin says. Guilt."

Vogel shrugged. "It's merely the most likely explanation for the bones, Susan. After all, slave owners buried slaves in what was then open ground - to avoid graveyard fees. Later on, when Cape Town needed to expand, they moved the white cemeteries, but the slave remains were simply built over."

He indicated the Slave Lodge, on the edge of Church Square. "No one knows where the Dutch East India Company buried its slaves - so, in fact, close by, right outside the first white cemetery, is the most likely spot of all."

"Edwin was quite hurt by Rafik's attitude," replied Susan. "He took it very personally, actually. You should have stuck up for him, darling. It's just religious fanaticism. Really you should. It's emotional blackmail, that's all."

"Oh, Rafi didn't altogether mean it, Susan. He was just sounding off."

"There you go, you see. Making excuses. Edwin was horrified."

"You have to understand Rafi, darling. He feels ... bruised." Vogel was astonished to hear himself using an endearment - something he did not usually permit himself - in his attempt to win Susan over in this dispute.

She had noticed this uncharacteristic slip, too. She pounced quickly. "It doesn't justify him being nasty. He and Edwin have been friends for ..."

The waitress appeared. She placed a coffee in front of Vogel and a glass of white wine before Susan, silently. Susan waited till she withdrew.

"Edwin was pretty upset that you didn't stand up for him," continued Susan softly. "You of all people. He felt horribly let down, in fact."

"I'm sorry," said Vogel. "Edwin has always taken things too much to heart. You know that. Should I ring him, do you think? After all, it's ..."

"It's a symptom of the times, Edwin says. People don't dare say what they think. We're just being browbeaten by people who shout the loudest."

"Rafi doesn't shout," objected Vogel. "He just feels, I don't know ..."

Vogel stared out at Church Square. "Excluded, I think."

"Excluded? That's absolute rot, Macaulay, and you know it!"

Over the hum of lunchtime traffic, the archivist could clearly hear the unremitting mantra of the protesters, led by metallic instruction through the megaphone. With a shock, he realized it was a woman's voice and that the crowd was now chanting in Afrikaans: "*Laat die geraamte bly ... Laat die geraamte slaap.*"

Susan leaned over and, needlessly, re-adjusted his open shirt collar. "Honestly, Macaulay, it's time to stop such special pleading now. Everyone says that Rafi's tour business is doing terribly well. Making pots of money."

Vogel remembered something that Rafik had said as they scrambled back down the mountain the previous Sunday. He had said it out of the blue, perhaps merely to ease the tension, to break their long drawn-out silence.

"Suzie," Vogel smiled at Susan affectionately. "Some slaves, you know, believed that the white man's shoes were made out of black skin."

Susan scanned the café impatiently. "For God's sake, no one can take this long to make a chicken mayo sandwich - not even in Cape Town."

"Susan," said Vogel urgently, louder than he had intended. He saw the look of unease in her grey-blue eyes. "Susan," he repeated softly, pleading.

"You're being very odd, Macaulay. Are you alright?"

Tears swelled in his own eyes. "Oh Suzie," he muttered, "Suzie …"

Susan's expression swiftly readjusted, changing to a flush of concern, almost motherly. Vogel bit his lip to hold back the tears, unable to speak.

Quickly he looked down at his cup and stirred the cold black coffee.

Susan reached across and squeezed his hand. "What is it, sweetheart?"

He hesitated. "Susan …"

"I love it when you say my name," she whispered.

"Susan, actually, the reason I asked you to meet me …"

"Yes?"

Vogel cleared his throat to control the unsteady quaver in his voice.

"Sweetheart," she said. "Tell me."

He laughed, embarrassed. "What do they say about me? Edwin, Rafik … the others. People who knew me in the past." He looked at her beseechingly. "Do they say anything about me, how I was then?"

"Gossip, you mean?"

"You know, what I was like … how I behaved, stuff like that."

Susan withdrew her hand. She glanced quickly round the café to see if anyone had noticed. Vogel waited until she looked back at him.

"Okay, for example … did I drink too much?"

He noticed Susan was toying absently with her wedding ring.

"Or do they say I was - look, I don't know … say, a womanizer?"

In the hush that followed Vogel became conscious of the yells from the demonstrators. He wondered if Susan was listening as she stared at him. They were chanting in English again: "Leave the bones, leave the bones."

"This is why you called this morning?" said Susan softly. "Summoned me from my work, urgently - to enquire if, in the good old days, you were known as a ladies' man?"

"No, no. It's not that." Vogel felt the conversation slipping away from him hopelessly. "Susan, I'm only trying to find out who ... what I was like."

"Look, I don't even want to know what you were like before," replied Susan. "Why are you doing this, Mac? There are some things we leave alone. You know that. Don't spoil it." She smiled fiercely. "Come on, darling, perk up. You're being very depressing."

"Sorry," said Vogel.

"Rather like a tedious archivist." Susan laughed. "It doesn't suit you."

"I'm unsettled, that's all." Vogel sighed. "You're right - it's probably working in the archives, sifting through layers and layers of stuff, trying to sort out trickery from the truth. It gets you down sometimes."

"You've been very odd lately, darling. Reclusive, not returning calls."

"You know, I thought I knew, pretty much, what I was. Okay, plenty of faults and all, but ... familiar, like an old photo. Now I'm not so sure."

"Macaulay," said Susan sharply, "what is this really about?"

"I look at myself twenty years ago and wonder - who the hell's that?"

"Please, darling, tell me this isn't some kind of mid-life crisis."

"Try to understand. I simply don't recognise this person at all. It's hard to explain, even to myself. It's very ... upsetting." He flapped his hands, self-deflatingly. "Perhaps I don't know what it means to be white anymore."

"Look, I wasn't there when you and Edwin and Rafi and the others were fighting the great fight and boozing and whoring or whatever else it was you were up to. But I've had enough of hearing about all that, thanks."

"Susan, this is important. It's been worrying - tormenting - me all week. I've thought a lot about this, Sue. And you're the only person ..."

"I already have one emotional cripple to look after," Susan Sarkissian interrupted swiftly. "You know that perfectly well, Mac."

She paused, composed. "I don't, ever, burden you with my ..."

She shrugged. "There you are, darling - don't push it."

Vogel felt his face flush. Without warning, a long-suppressed craving bubbled up; a molten desire to confide, and for intimacy, sluiced through him. Furtive tears of self-pity moistened the archivist's pleading eyes again.

"Anyhow," Susan smiled brightly. "Tell me about your work."

Vogel struggled to keep his voice level. He told her about the find of police files: the call from Deputy Minister D.K. Biyela; how he had been allocated a room in the Castle, secluded from tourists, a small wood-lined military storeroom with minute square windows; that he was thus under the control of the military, and how this room was now stacked with documents, haphazard and disorderly, out of which he was expected to make some order.

"Isn't this a state secret?" Susan asked playfully.

Vogel told her about discovering his own file.

"Is that all?" she asked, amused. "Is that what all this fuss is about?"

"Suzie, I have no idea who this person is, you see - no idea at all."

"Does it contain secrets, revelations ... intimacies?"

"No. Just dates, lists of meetings, events I attended, people I knew." Vogel hesitated. "And some ... observations."

"Observations?"

"Comments. Personal remarks about my character."

"Then what's the problem?"

"I'm not sure if that was really me. Or just what people thought."

He locked into her cool gaze, beseeching. "Susan, I want to know. Macaulay Vogel ... was that honestly, truly him? I need to know, you see."

"Mac, you can't torment yourself about what someone once thought of you, especially that long ago. And the security police, for heaven's sake! What does it matter anyway? It's history. Move on, Mac. Most of the bad guys have. They carry on with regular lives. Things change. But you, the rebels, the good guys ... you're trapped. You can't let go, can you? You hug the past. Cling onto it, like grasping at wreckage. Edwin, Rafik - you're all the same. You *hoard* the past. This is a sickness. You know that, don't you?"

"But what if ... if I wasn't who I've always thought I was, at all? I mean, if I don't recognize this person, this specific individual called

Macaulay Vogel, then maybe what other people were saying about him ..."

Even as he was speaking Vogel noticed the change in her eyes.

"This is about something else altogether, isn't it?" said Susan sharply.

"No, I'm just trying to find out ..."

"You're trying to find out if there was an informer." The startling grey-blue of her gaze turned opaque. "That's what all this is about, really."

"Susan, I only want to understand ..."

"You suspect it's Edwin, don't you?" Her voice was quick and angry. "Oh my! You're not upset by any crazy identity stuff at all. You're actually trying to pry out of me if my husband gave away information about you."

Vogel had once, several years before, right at the start of their affair, asked Susan about Edwin, about the time that he had been detained by the police for interrogation and tortured. She had told him then, sharply, that it was none of his business. The phrase she had used, and repeated whenever Vogel mentioned Edwin, was that he must "mind his P's and Q's." Susan had met and married Edwin not long after his release from prison, and in the nineteen years since she'd drawn an increasingly protective veil around him, shielding Edwin from the concern of his comrades and the pity of outsiders.

"How dare you suspect your oldest friend." Susan's tone was cold, deadpan. "Have you no self respect? My God, Macaulay, you're behaving like a secret policeman yourself. Prying, snooping, deceiving, cynical. Yes, you learnt their lessons well. It's poisoned you, contaminated everything."

Her controlled voice quivered slightly, "I might as well accuse you."

Susan paused for a moment, to let the charge penetrate, without taking her eyes off him. Vogel stared back, mesmerized, unable to find any words.

"And if you're going to point the finger at friends who were tortured, why not start with Billy?" she continued dispassionately. "Or even ..."

Vogel felt leaden, submissive, uninvolved. Susan's words sounded

49

remote, as though he were eavesdropping on someone else's conversation.

At first it didn't seem to refer to him when she added, "After all, no one knew more about Macaulay Vogel than her. So why not Marda, hm?"

The waitress arrived, bearing two plates. "Here we go," she beamed.

Susan rose unhurriedly and smiled back, "Good, and here I go, too."

"But your lunch, m'am?"

"Oh," replied Susan amiably. "I'm sure Dr. Vogel can manage that."

Vogel watched Susan walk rapidly to the door. As always she looked elegant and poised. The waitress hovered, uncertain, then placed one plate in front of Vogel and the other in the empty place opposite him.

"Will there be anything else, sir?" she enquired.

Vogel stared out of the window. Indistinctly he heard the rhythmic chant, "*Laat die geraamte slaap*." He gazed blankly at Church Square and the Slave Lodge. It wasn't possible. He had known everything about Marda. She had never been detained, let alone tortured.

Susan had once remarked to him, early on, in an uncharacteristically personal aside, after they'd had some furious, inconsequential row: "How on earth do you think it feels, Macaulay, to be the second of Sarkissian's wives also to become your mistress?" He remembered how at the time the word 'mistress' had sounded so outlandish to his ears, quaintly old-fashioned and jarring. It hadn't occurred to him at first that she was referring to Marda.

He had always thought of Marda as his wife.

Then, when he didn't react, Susan added, "I know people say that I even look like Marda. So how do you think it feels, Mac? To know that I've stepped into her shoes, the second Mrs. Edwin Sarkissian to be ..."

Susan hadn't completed the sentence. They didn't discuss the matter further. Vogel never pried about Edwin; Susan remained silent about Marda.

Vogel became aware that Susan was standing next to him, by the table.

"I'm sorry," she said.

She remained standing. "I should never have said that about Marda."

Susan was embarrassed. "But, Macaulay, you've turned your home into a mausoleum. You're so self-absorbed. Do you know how that feels?"

Vogel stared at her.

"Your home is like your heart … closed."

Vogel was aware of people at other tables staring at them curiously.

"Macaulay, you asked me if you were, for example, a womanizer?"

Before she turned to depart, Susan bent down and kissed him swiftly on the lips. There were tears, he noticed, in her eyes.

"The fact is, darling, you've used women to harden your heart."

Eight

THERE was not a curl or lick of wind off the sea. Accumulated heat, trapped by the mountain, compressed down on the torpid city. There had been no rain for five months. In the suburbs, gardens wilted. The Castle grew hushed, almost deserted. Vogel noticed even the guards stayed indoors.

The glare of the sun was sweaty and insinuating. Nerves wore ragged, taxis hooted louder. Night brought no relief. Another bomb went off under cover of dark, this time near the station. It had been placed at the base of the statue of Maria de la Queillerie. The bomb, largely packed with petrol, created an impressive detonation and took several sizeable chunks out of the sandstone pedestal, but the bronze figure itself survived unscathed. Maria had been the wife of the first Dutch commander at the Cape and his statue was only meters away. Vogel wondered why Van Riebeeck's spouse had been targeted instead. Like the explosion in the docks, this attack remained anonymous. Was it an assault on a symbol of power, hatred for colonisation and the first white settlers? Or was this simply an eruption of misogyny?

Vogel worked late at the Castle every evening. His constricted room, stuffed with files, was roasting. The boxy windows, he discovered, would not open. Outside, with dusk and a starry sky, the air still felt as sticky and breathless. By the time Vogel reached the flower market most vendors had packed up and several times, out of a sorrowing ache, he had bought up all the flowers that were left. One evening, his arms overflowing with a profuse bouquet of phlox and cannas, the archivist got caught up in a large march at the top of Adderley Street, heading for Parliament.

At the front were men in jalabiyyas and women, despite the heat, wrapped in shawls and scarves. Following behind were hundreds of workmen in blue and orange overalls, as if they had come straight from building sites. They carried familiar placards and were yelling the same monotonous slogan: "Leave the bones, let the bones sleep."

As the crowd stopped outside the Slave Lodge, facing Parliament, they spread across Adderley Street and disrupted the traffic. Vogel, trying to push through the dense mass, suddenly felt smothered. He experienced an unreasoning surge of rage and disgust. They were shouting and furiously waving fists at an empty building. What did these people want?

Vogel elbowed his way through the crowd and, irrationally unnerved by resentment and lonely guilt, hurried home as fast as he could.

The files in his office at the Castle seemed to inflate and multiply. The already overcrowded room, with creaking floorboards and splintered shutters, seemed to shrink every day. Documents appeared now to reach, even touch, the low ceiling. To Vogel, it was as if those folders and dossiers replicated in his nighttime absence and that, when he returned in the morning, there were forever added reports, piling up in an alarming disarray. The more he moved the files around in his desperate search, the less order he felt he was able to impose and the more those records seemed to proliferate. The tiny office was stuffy, baking. The files hemmed him in, seeming to absorb all the available oxygen, threatening to suffocate the archivist in a cascade of untamed words. Occasionally he came across the name of someone who had tenuously been connected to his group and he rifled through these reports eagerly. Vogel skimmed pages, not even attempting to interpret their content. He was searching only for one word, and every word on every page was never that word. His eyes glazed with sweat, exhaustion and obsession and all that Vogel saw after a while was that no word was ever the name that he craved.

On three successive nights he arrived home late to find messages on his answer phone from Mary Xaba, inviting him to dinner, repeating that she and Zechariah were worried they had not heard from him. He did not reply.

One evening, with instant elation, he came across a startling folder. On the cover was the name Sivuyile wakwa Gqabe. He'd somehow missed this when he had sifted through that same stack a dozen times already. Vogel felt so agitated he could barely permit himself to open it. This dossier, he was convinced, would yield up the intangible clue for which he had been searching. Here, finally, could be that elusive word; the name he had sought with such desperation. It had been Sivuyile who introduced him to Marda.

He stared at the cover uneasily. Sivuyile had also, he remembered, first introduced Edwin to Marda. She had in fact been the liaison between their group and the black lawyer in Bisho. Stamped on the grubby beige cover was the case reference number: B28C ... what, he wondered, did that code mean? Sivuyile was renowned as a ladies man, he reflected, and was struck by a random thought: had Marda had an affair with Sivuyile? To smother his guilt at this suspicion, Vogel opened the folder. It was empty.

Vogel had always comforted himself that he'd known everything about Marda. Now it felt as though he were staring into a void. There were, it seemed, no words left. There was no written testimony or verification to confirm their bond, to cross-reference or vouch for their love. He could not even hope, apparently, for any irrefutable evidence to at least corroborate or disprove Susan's confident assertion that Marda had been detained and tortured. The words had shrivelled, like petals, and simply evaporated.

Data, testimonies, including evidence from potential witnesses, appeared to melt away even as he reached out to where he might reasonably except to locate them. Initially Vogel had pointed out to Deputy Minister Biyela that many records were also likely to have been stored on computer disks and hard drives. "Deleted," replied Minister Biyela with a laugh.

How could he possibly not have known if Marda had been arrested, let alone tortured? The thought itself tormented him. If he didn't know that, what else did he not know? Was he so self-absorbed that he had simply, somehow, not noticed ... or had Marda perhaps - so typical of her - been protecting him? Susan, of course, could be lying: jealous, trying to hurt him.

The incredulity, the doubt and uncertainty was raw. It undermined everything Vogel had imagined he believed in; that gave his life meaning. The less he feared he knew about Marda, the less he felt he knew himself.

He re-doubled his labours, frantically scrutinizing the same files, but words simply blurred, isolated and futile, never the ones that he longed for.

On Saturday, when he returned from the Castle, there was a brief message from Zechariah. "Mac," said the familiar gruff voice. "Call."

Vogel telephoned on Sunday when he knew they would be out, taking Zech's mother to church in Guguletu. "Hey, I'm fine," he chided, affecting cheeriness. "Busy as hell though. I'll be in contact soon as I'm clear. *Ciao*."

The following day, after another futile hunt among the files, Vogel left the Castle after nightfall. It was nearly eleven o'clock. He took the short cut down Plein, and as he approached Spin Street he saw a small gathering of protesters. They now maintained a twenty-four hour vigil around the site. It was dark. As he passed by the hushed group and crossed the road he heard a shout. "Macaulay!" Without the distorting vibration of a megaphone, he recognised the voice immediately. Vogel hurried on, pretending not to hear.

"Macaulay," yelled the rasping voice, louder. "Macaulay Vogel!"

The archivist increased his pace and moved closer to the barricaded shops, away from the street lighting. Within moments he was swallowed into the shadows. Behind him he thought he heard a collective murmur, a long-drawn out sigh. Immediately he felt ashamed of himself. It was, however, too late to turn back. He couldn't be sure. He might have even imagined this. But when Vogel thought about it later, and it was as if he could still hear that pained susurration, he thought it sounded like a collective hiss of disgust.

When that scratchy, rabble-rousing voice had yelled his name Vogel had been under the trees on the traffic isle in the middle of Spin Street; in fact as he scurried down the deserted pavement the archivist realized, with a thump of guilt, that he had been right next to the plaque which recorded the site of the slave tree, under which slaves in Cape Town had once been sold.

Vogel thought of what Rafik had whispered, out of Edwin's hearing, as they had trudged despondently back down the mountain in hostile silence.

"You know, for nearly a hundred years slaves were in the majority here," Rafik grumbled, "and today ... man, it's like they never existed."

Then, angrily: "And still we're treated like second class citizens."

It was true. Apart from the Slave Lodge and the small plaque in Spin Street, which most people walked past without a second glance, slavery had effectively been erased from the map and from memory, though invisibly it drew most of the social contours that still divided the city. As Vogel turned the corner into his street he felt ashamed. Having moments ago turned away from an old comrade like Marc Hendricks, he'd denied his own past, too.

The archivist opened the bright yellow door to his home in Sabata Dalindyebo Way, but he did not experience his usual sense of relief. The house seemed strange to him, cold, not the sanctuary of peace and refuge he had known all his life. His mother had been absurdly proud of their house and street. "Yonge Street is named after the British Governor Sir George Yonge," she boasted regularly. Nadira had so tenaciously delighted in their colonial heritage that, much later, when she was old, Vogel did not have the heart to tell her that Sir George had been recalled to Britain in disgrace.

The fact that the name Yonge had been expunged from this narrow, insignificant street, and been replaced by Sabata Dalindyebo Way, would have disoriented Nadira completely. The past, even his own, was by degrees being overlaid. In recent years neighboring houses had not only been re-painted, but most sprouted new burglar bars and alarm systems, while some of the balconies were also topped with razor wire. Inexorably it seemed the history of who he was and had been was gradually being rendered invisible.

Nine

THE cruel heat eased slightly and Vogel returned to examining the files in his room at the Castle more methodically. In the evenings, rather than return to his broiling house, the archivist took to roaming the streets. He'd always walked his city. Now in the dusk he sensed, almost palpably, that Cape Town still retained many of the blemishes from its origins as a half-way refreshment station to the East: tavern and brothel ... indolent, sensuous, buffeted by trade winds, forever populated by masters and vassals.

Vogel had walked Cape Town all his life and imagined he could feel the layers of the neglected past rise up under his feet, like an archive of the city. When he looked at black and white photos on display in museums, frozen in sepia like remote historical tableaux - pictures of ocean liners with crowds on the quayside throwing streamers or cobbled street scenes of the pitilessly demolished District Six or black political prisoners being ferried in shackles to Robben Island - Vogel felt dizzied by the potency of that past. These were things that he remembered like a living presence.

During daylight hours he continued with a more orderly search, but as he tramped the darkening streets late into the night, Vogel recognised that his obsessive rifling through the files was futile. He knew that for what he was seeking he would have to rely on human sources and memories. After several days' indecision, Vogel rang Rafik.

The telephone rang a dozen times. Vogel feared that "Billy" might answer. If he did, Vogel had decided to hang up. Eventually Rafik picked up.

At first his friend was unresponsive. It was not a good time, he said. This was still the high tourist season, and they had several tours every day. He was far too busy.

Vogel persisted. "It's important," he said. "This won't take long, I promise. Half an hour, max."

He added: "I'll come to your office."

"No," answered Rafik swiftly. "Not the office. Our house, tomorrow morning at eight o' clock."

Rafik and Billy had moved several months previously from an outlying suburb to the Bo-Kaap, on the cobbled slopes of Signal Hill, at the western edge of the city centre. At the time Rafik had been faintly embarrassed. "Yup," he'd laughed, "as you see, we're trading up." Bo-Kaap remained a largely Muslim area with several mosques. But the diminutive, brightly painted Cape Dutch and Georgian cottages were rapidly becoming fashionable, attracting middle-class outsiders and affluent foreigners. Vogel had not previously been invited to visit their new home. The next morning it took him twenty-five minutes to walk across town. Traffic was stalled on Buitengracht. As soon as Vogel climbed the steps to the Bo-Kaap, however, the city din muted. Seagulls swirled overhead. He sauntered up a steep street and found the brilliant orange façade in a restored row of terraced cottages.

Rafik was waiting at the front door. He led Vogel down a shadowed passageway, with rooms to either side. There was a soft mutter of a chiding female voice and through the half-open door of a darkened room, Vogel caught a brief glimpse of a woman leaning over a seated man, who was enveloped in a blanket. As he hurriedly followed Rafik down the corridor, Vogel was sure that this must have been Rafik's sister Roshana and "Billy".

Rafik opened the door at the end of the corridor and ushered Vogel into a dappled courtyard. A spray of scented jasmine covered the opposite wall, and to their left, under the shadow of a vine-threaded lattice, a small fountain played. Next to it were two wicker chairs and a silver tray with a pair of china cups. Freshly-brewed coffee had already been poured.

Vogel was nervous. Rafik had barely said a word and the contrast between the bright courtyard and his fleeting sight of the two indistinct figures inside disturbed him.

"What do you want?" asked Rafik, as he pointed to a chair.

Vogel silently accepted a coffee. He looked around the sedate, cool courtyard - ochre walls, terracotta pots - and reflected that their tour business must be prospering. Fifteen years ago Rafik and "Billy" had set up a company called "Alternative Adventures." The novelty was to take tourists away from the usual colonial sights to another reality: of black townships, District Six and Bo-Kaap. They also offered what Rafik scoffingly referred to as "Struggle Safaris", a tour of sites where the army or police had engaged in battle - either with thousands of protestors, often school children, or with armed resistance fighters. This was to have been Billy's responsibility, as he had been a commander of an underground unit, but steadily over the years as his nerves buckled he had become increasingly reclusive. Although never talked about openly in their circle, it was supposed that Billy was completely house-bound. Vogel knew, however, that he could not possibly ask Rafik.

He smiled. "For our climb this Sunday," he began cheerily. "I thought we might try Skeleton Gorge. Haven't done that for a while, have we?"

Rafik stared impassively back.

"It's going to be boiling," added Vogel. "So Skeleton Gorge would be best, with lots of shade."

"I don't think so," replied Rafik flatly. "Not after what Edwin said last time."

Vogel hesitated. This wasn't the point of his visit, yet already he was caught up in discord. He shrugged. "Agh, Edwin didn't mean anything."

"Fundamentalists? Zealots? Hey, you heard him."

"Sure, but that's just Edwin sounding off."

"He obviously assumes that Billy and I have become ..."

"Rafi, this is a friendship that goes way back. After all we've been through!"

"That doesn't give Sarkissian" - members of their tight circle had long ago latched onto the convention of calling Edwin by his surname, a practice carried over from his private boarding school days - "the right to insult me. He as good as said that Billy and I are some kind of religious fanatics."

"He's ... excitable. Sure, Edwin overreacts. You know that."

"Yeah? Well, it also sounds like what you're saying is that the people who've been wronged must, as usual, forgive."

"Rafi, the man's got problems. He's nervy, gets far too emotional."

"And don't think I don't know exactly what Sarkissian says about our tour business too." Rafik grimaced. "He calls it poverty tourism."

"Surely not!" Vogel affected surprise. "No, I've never heard ..."

"Please, Mac - don't make excuses. This stuff gets back to me. He's an architect. Sarkissian restores colonial buildings. Victorian, that's what he likes. So showing people wretched shanty towns ... well, he's right in a way. It is a sort of, 'wow, look at these pitiful folk' sightseeing. But frankly, when we started our business, poverty was the only resource Billy and I had."

Rafik paused. "Maybe we're not yet affluent enough to have your scruples."

Then, with a laugh: "We're branching out, though - beginning to take tourists to the winelands, too. You know, townships and grinding poverty in the morning, then a thirty minute drive for a fine lunch at some gracious wine estate in Stellenbosch or Paarl. Foreigners love the combination. We market this as, 'explore the two South Africas in one day.' It's very popular. It's also a lot more expensive, of course." He waved his arm to take in the sunlit courtyard. "You white folk showed us the way - sure, poverty pays. And that's what made it possible for us to move from Rylands to Bo-Kaap."

The courtyard was quiet. There was no indication of the heat or clamour in the city. Vogel heard a soft lament of gulls. A gecko darted up the wall and into the jasmine. He wondered how to bring the conversation round to the reason for his visit. For the moment Rafik seemed to have forgotten yesterday's barbed assertion that he was too busy.

Vogel, drowsy in the stippled sunlight, thought of the shrouded figure indoors, cosseted in the shadows.

"Sarkissian doesn't understand," declared Rafik abruptly, breaking the lethargic silence. "This isn't about facts. It isn't about science or testing or whatever. It's about what we feel. I mean, for instance, some slaves used to think the white man's cheese was made from black

62

brains. But Sarkissian? He doesn't care about our feelings. He thinks they're just a few old bones. No, man, those were people, slaves … our people. See, what we feel is that white people don't care. They just want to dig them up, push them around, pull and poke those bones, like they was nothing!"

Vogel was so startled at this anger that he didn't know how to respond.

"It's like we're invisible, too - yes, that's how it feels." Rafik sighed. "And you didn't even stick up for me, Mac. Don't think I didn't notice."

Vogel breathed in a sweet, tender scent of jasmine. Against the pale lilac tiles he noticed that fallen blossoms had turned sun-singed and squishy.

The sun had moved higher, pouring more amber brilliance into the courtyard. Above, the cobalt sky glowed; the salt-scoured air was moist and fresh. On crystalline days such as this Vogel remembered playing chess with Rafik in the shaded café in the Gardens: a rare no man's land of anonymity in the rigid segregation of the past, where they could converse undisturbed, ostensibly absorbed in their game, while Vogel passed on messages.

"God, don't you miss that sometimes, Rafi," said Vogel. "The clarity of the past. How everything seemed so stark and simple - the decisions we were faced with, actions one had to take. Everything was more … definite."

"You're nostalgic?" Rafik asked incredulously. "You miss all that? Is that what you wanted to talk about? To reminisce about the old days?"

"Good heavens, of course not!' Vogel felt a shiver of irritation. It was as if his friend was deliberately trying to misinterpret everything that he said. "No, I'm just saying that, you know, somehow, in the past … every moment one was faced with crucial moral decisions. It was clear to us what was right and what was evil. There was a precise choice. There was an intensity about our life then - a certainty of purpose. Now things are more … complicated. Nothing anymore is quite as …"

"Exciting?"

"No! Straightforward."

Vogel knew he was floundering. Rafik looked at him blankly. The archivist experienced a bristle of annoyance. He had always thought his friend had remained unscathed by the years, with his smooth, amiable, fleshy face, and slightly portly build, but now it seemed to Vogel there was a stocky complacency, even an inflexibility and stubbornness that he had not detected before. He was sure Rafik knew exactly what he meant, and was deliberately trying to make him feel uncomfortable, or even provoke him.

The conversation was going hopelessly wrong. Every time Vogel tried a new tack, Rafik seemed purposefully to block him, like a crafty - possibly spiteful - chess stratagem. It was as though this middle-aged man, staring back coolly, was completely unfamiliar.

"Don't you ever wonder, Rafi, who that person was back then - you know, the fearless young man with all that energy and reckless passion?"

Ten, even five years ago, Vogel reflected, Rafik would have scorned the idea of treating a cache of unidentified bones as sacred relics. He would have dismissed such an attitude as archaic. Once, he'd ardently repudiated any suggestion that his identity was carved by pigment, ancestry or religion. Then, as Vogel remembered from many discussions, Rafik identified himself as rational, strictly secular, progressive and socialist. Ten years ago Rafik would have mocked the idea of defining himself primarily as a Muslim.

Vogel answered his own question. "I do," he continued. "These days I often wonder … who, actually, was that person I used to be, twenty years ago? I don't know anymore. Am I the same … or have I changed?"

"Is that, really, why you came to see me?" asked Rafik quietly.

Vogel smiled with relief. He was overreacting. Rafik was a friend; a confidant, a comrade. Rafik would know. Rafik would tell him the

" he said. "The thing is, I'm just not sure any longer what person I used to be. Know what I mean? It could be anything, Like, did people really trust me? And my behaviour … or, say, too impulsive? Perhaps I was a bit of an I drank too much? You've known me as well as

64

anyone, Rafi. Better! What did people really say about me? I mean, was I regarded as completely trustworthy, for example? Or was I a bit egotistical? You know … too self-centered?"

"Susan rang, warned me you might want to see me," replied Rafik.

"Susan? Susan Sarkissian?"

"She said you'd been given security police files to examine and …"

"Susan told you that? She had no right to! That's strictly - officially - classified."

"Ah, we're such good buddies, eh, except now - oh, shame - there are some secrets?" Rafik spoke slowly. "You want me to disclose confidences to you, Macaulay, but suddenly your files are confidential?"

Vogel was indignant. "And why the hell are you talking to Susan Sarkissian anyway? After what happened on the mountain with Edwin, I would have thought …"

"Susan and I understand each other, we have troubles in common," responded Rafik. "And she was right. Susan said you'd come to badger me about those files."

"That's just because I …" Unexpectedly, just as he had in the café with Susan, Vogel felt he was on the threshold of tears. "That's because this person in the file, Macaulay Vogel, isn't a person I remember at all."

"That's not what Susan says," declared Rafik. "No, Susan says that you came across your own police dossier there and want to find out who leaked information about you."

"Rafi, it's not true," gasped the archivist. "There's just stuff in there - about myself - that I can't identify as me, so I'm only trying to find out …"

"You're trying to find the informer. Admit it, Mac. Susan told me you'd accused Sarkissian. She warned me you'd suspect Billy next."

Instantly Vogel grasped what Rafik had meant by saying that he and Susan Sarkissian had troubles in common. Both their partners, of course, had been detained by the security police and tortured. Billy's suffering had been much longer and far worse. "Billy" had been his code name, and everyone had continued to use it ever since, so that Vogel could no longer even recall Billy's real name. It was possible he'd never known his given name in the first place. He thought of the

huddled figure indoors, concealed in shadows. It was simply Billy -
Billy and Rafik, as if they had always been a pair.

Vogel had been on one of their 'Struggle Safaris' and the one thing
that had never been mentioned was the most dramatic. They'd passed
close to the street in Nyanga, but had not stopped at the scene where
eight young men had died when the police had stormed the house in the
early hours of the morning. The police had shot seven of them while they
were still asleep in their beds, and the survivor they'd hunted through the
ill-lit streets, clothed only in pants and shoes and unarmed, until they
cornered him in a cul-de-sac and, although the teenager put his hands
up to surrender, his police pursuers had executed him anyway. "Billy"
had been in prison at the time and it was assumed that the police had
extracted their information from him. This had never been confirmed,
however, nor the details of Billy's torture. Subsequently the memory
of that slaughter had largely been erased from the record - and from
Rafik's tour - while Billy had, over the years, declined into a recluse.

He was cared for now by Rafik's sister Roshana. She also acted as an
opportune and plausible chaperone, which conveniently allowed their
neighbours in a traditionally conservative community to collude with
sly tolerance in the fiction that Billy and she were the real couple.

"The trouble is," said Rafik, rising, "you always blame us. Every
time, you think we are the weak point. You whites, you've no idea.
Like tourists."

His voice was quivering with anger. "Well, Mac, I'm not going to
allow you to blame Billy. Hear me? Billy is a good man."

Rafik was standing. "I'm going to ask you to leave," he stated
calmly.

"No, Rafi, please listen, this is important ..."

"Now," announced Rafik, turning quickly.

They walked hurriedly back down the dark corridor. The house
was silent. The side door, which had been half open before, was closed.
There was a renewed growl of traffic and blinding sunlight in the steep
street.

Vogel said urgently, "Rafi, there was stuff about Marda, too. I ..."

"Billy's a good man," repeated Rafik. "Don't ever come back, you
hear?"

Ten

OUT in the Atlantic, a storm lashed. Jade-green swells surged over hundreds of kilometers to pound kelp and marine waste onto beaches of the exposed peninsula. In Cape Town, however, the late March heat wallowed.

When Vogel took a lonely hike up Signal Hill on Sunday his shoes scuffed powdery billows of sand from the seared grass. There was a thin resinous scent of pine. Overhead the flinty African sky was constricted only by a provincial horizon of enfolding, dust-brown hills.

Turning away from the ocean, to his right, even the normally luxuriant emerald strip of the botanical gardens looked russet and parched. Late on Friday night another minor bomb had exploded, right in the centre of the old Dutch East India Company Gardens, at the foot of the statue to Cecil Rhodes. On the plinth, a metal plate with the inscription, 'Cecil John Rhodes, 1853-1902,' had been blown away. But the life-size statue itself was barely singed, so that the crumpled imperialist still faced north, streaks of verdigris on his chubby face like runnels of sweat, left arm raised high, pointing to the rest of Africa. The bomb, Vogel assumed, had been intended to eradicate this invitation to extend the British empire all the way to Cairo, for also emblazoned on the demolished plaque had been the exhortation, "Your hinterland is there", as if the white settlers should simply sweep through the continent, appropriating anything they wanted.

Earlier colonists had already done so in the Cape. When the first Europeans had arrived, there were people living there with names for everything: the mountain, the bay, rivers, streams, forests, hills and pastures. The Dutch had simply wiped this evidence, literally, off their maps. It was as if by re-naming, they could acquire dominion over all they surveyed. Around him now mostly English classifications remained. As Vogel turned slowly, west to east, he took in Bantry Bay, Sea Point, Three Anchor Bay and the Victoria and Alfred Waterfront, named after the English Queen and a son who had visited the southern tip of Africa. One of the rare place names to have been altered, Sabata Dalindyebo Way, was too tiny to see. Even the castle, he reflected, was squeezed between Strand Street and Darling.

Despite the opinion that he professed to his friends, Vogel found this constancy reassuring. Further north, when landmarks, towns or rivers were re-designated with a local African name, most of the white people became extremely agitated as if their entire universe was being upended. Now, as he surveyed the sloping confines of his city - Signal Hill, Lion's Head, Devil's Peak - he was comforted by those cherished summits and contours of his childhood. Simply repeating the words to himself brought the archivist a sense of peace, like reciting a sacred litany. Table Mountain, Muizenberg, Woodstock, Observatory, Loop Street, Long Street, Adderley Street ... the names were lulling. The familiar words themselves, packed with meaning and richness, soothed him: supple petals of memory.

After his bruising encounter with Rafik, Vogel had retreated behind the broad stone ramparts of the Castle. The archivist sought refuge again in the files. As always in times of crisis or disappointment, he turned back to the written records - to his faith in words, in the hope that this would restore to him a lost sense of coherence and meaning. But his methodical search only confirmed that he could find no order in these documents. There was no sign of his 'personal' file; and the more he looked, the more it wasn't there.

On Wednesday afternoon, after further discouraging sticky hours with the files, Vogel returned home early in order to telephone Grethe Cilliers. It had not been as easy to make an appointment with her as he had hoped. Vogel had been pleasantly encouraged to discover that although Grethe was now a household celebrity, she was still listed in the telephone directory. But when he'd phoned her home number an African maid answered.

"Madam is out," she informed him. "Madam is in the office."

Vogel was astonished to find himself state: "Madam's office number, please."

He spoke to three secretaries and a production assistant before being given an appointment to telephone the following morning, at ten thirty. Vogel remained at home and called on the exact minute. He was kept waiting for nearly half an hour, listening to loops of Vivaldi mixed with a recorded woman's voice: "Your call is important ..."

"Macaulay," suddenly interrupted another trilling voice. "Precious!"

"Grethe ..."

"Sweetheart, I've been in the studio, recording. But, Mac, how long's it been? Eleven ... twelve years? Why don't you ever call me, sweetie?"

Grethe was unable to find a gap in her schedule the next day or over the weekend.

"Bloody television, it's a tyrant, don't you agree? We're shooting a new series right now and ... no, darling, I wouldn't dream of you trekking to the office. You'll come and have lunch with me at home. Just the two of us. You haven't been to my new house, Macaulay? That's hideously remiss of you, *skattie*. Then Monday's a must."

Vogel drove out of Cape Town in his aged, panting blue Peugeot. The archivist had set off in good time to ensure a prompt arrival and traffic on the N2 was light. To his left, in the field next to the twin concrete towers of Athlone power station, he noticed several make-shift plastic huts. These were for young Xhosa males, the *abakhwetha*, who were unable to go into the bush for their ceremonial initiation into manhood. He hadn't left the confines of the city and yet flanking each other - unnoticed by most commuters who sped by every day - co-existed this astonishing contrast of modernity and tradition.

Vogel continued past the airport and immense shack megalopolis of Khayelitsha, ever-expanding despite being marooned on the sandy plain between motorway and ocean. He stayed parallel to the light curve of the coast and, following Grethe's directions, turned off the N2 after Somerset West, climbing into the stony, saw-toothed hills overlooking False Bay.

Soon he came to a private gravel road with the sign: 'Living the

Tuscan lifestyle.' Springing up all over the peninsula were high-walled, enclosed estates with names like Montebello, Sabbioneta and Miramare.

At the summit of the rise, like a huddled Italian hill town, stood the security complex 'Girasole', a cluster of red-tiled houses surrounded by a towering ochre wall. At the electronic gateway a guard saluted. He checked Vogel's name on his register.

Inside, the narrow streets were cobbled. Each almost identical two-storied villa was set in an expanse of well-trimmed lawn, bordered with cheerful flower beds. Wooden signposts led Vogel to the tastefully blanched terracotta tints of 'Casa Cilliers'. As he ascended the marble steps, leading to a spacious terrace and Georgian front door, a black maid in white pinafore was already waiting for him.

She announced, "Sir is twenty minutes early."

"I prefer to be early," replied Vogel amiably. He pointed to a gardener, kneeling in a bed of flourishing columbine. "No water problems here, eh?"

The maid curtsied, "Madam will not be long. Madam is out jogging."

Vogel could see the entire expanse of False Bay, sun-flecked wavelets hemmed by bluish mountains tapering, in a daze of moist heat, to Cape Point. He remembered the day he'd broken off with Grethe, solemnly informing her that he had "lost his heart", though not telling her it was to her friend Marda; he remembered, too, how Grethe had laughed carelessly.

"Congratulations, precious," she'd cooed. "I'd begun to worry if you really had a heart," and then his absurd jealousy when Grethe proceeded to make clear that, anyway, she'd already slept with everyone else in their group, including Edwin and Sivuyile.

She had been irresistibly, unconventionally attractive, the bold poetess and temptress, and though Vogel had not watched her TV show, Grethe's picture was often in the *Cape Times*: face fuller, but still with that uniquely craggy bone structure and audacious stare. He'd last seen her at a birthday party for Lenny Barr nine years ago, when newspapers no longer referred to 'the precocious Afrikaans poetess' but 'a feared, *femme fatale* wine critic.'

"Macaulay ... you're always early, damn you!"

A broad woman in black Lycra shorts and bra bounded up the steps. "How sweet, couldn't wait to see me, you haven't changed a bit, precious."

Grethe Cilliers seemed double the size, as if her body had been rudely commandeered, leaving only a ghostly allusion to her former silhouette. Her once untamed hair was cut mannishly short. Tight black running shorts and running bra exposed a muscled midriff and beefy shoulders. Grethe pressed his body to her. Vogel felt a powerful shock of warm, solid flesh.

Her face was flushed and soaked with sweat. Vogel inhaled a heady mix of fresh perspiration and expensive, musky perfume. He let himself be enveloped in her powerful clasp. She exuded the same impulsive audacity and raw physical vigor. Vogel felt a sub-sonic quiver of instant desire.

"Give me five minutes to change, sweetie," she exhaled. "Time, alas, is my tyrant, Mac ... I'm a bloody slave to notoriety. Sadly, darling, we've only got half an hour for lunch."

Grethe now owned her own television production company, but it was her rapid progression from wine expert to TV cook that had propelled her into the limelight. Vogel examined the photos in her silk-draped, airy living room. There were several of Grethe with well-known personalities who had appeared on her show, including an archbishop. Every newspaper profile lauded Grethe's heroic role in the past, though never mentioning Vogel. Together they had encoded secret messages, either from biblical verses or by jumbling words which they then divided into arbitrary lines, so that if caught while conveying a clandestine communication from city to city, Grethe could claim the incriminating evidence as one of her bold modernist poems.

It had been Grethe, he recalled, who had coined the term 'black petals.' This was their private code for the individual words which they had to isolate and jiggle around - detaching those units from any previous context or meaning, then reconfiguring a totally new sense and order by shuffling the very same words into a concealed yet decipherable system.

This allowed them to say, on the phone, "I'm studying flower arranging tonight." Or, "There's a surprise demand for black petals in Durban." In fact, Vogel was sure they'd once captioned one of their clandestine messages 'Black Petals', so that it really would look like a verse - or had that, actually, been the title of one of Grethe's published poems?

Grethe called from the terrace, "*Kom, skattie*," clapping her hands. She was seated at a small oval table, set for two, under a canvass awning. The maid hovered nearby. "Wine please, Phindiswa."

Grethe wore a saffron silk shirt, stretched taut. She made no attempt to hide her girth, instead emphasizing that full, rippling body. Vogel sat beside her, awkwardly tempted to reach out and fondle her springy flesh.

He said instead, "I was just remembering black petals, Grethe. I often imagine, as I'm examining a new file, that it is full of black petals."

"Black petals?" She hoisted a curried shrimp with her fingers and chewed hungrily. "What on earth are they, Mac?"

"Words, our code for words," he grinned, following her example with a slippery shrimp. "You wrote a poem called 'Black Petals', I'm sure."

"Not me, Mac." Grethe avidly sucked the mayonnaise and curry off her fingers. "Memory's playing up, sweetheart. No, sounds like one of your crazy ideas. I'd never dabble with such an ambiguous expression. I mean, these days that could even seem offensive, especially when we're trying to get away from obsessions with pigment, black or white, brown or whatever."

Grethe tilted her head inquisitively, teasing. Vogel was suddenly self-conscious. He wanted to lean across and stroke the granules of her skin.

Instead, "What was I like?" he blurted, "The person you knew?"

He was aware that his face had flushed. Grethe, however, nodded solemnly. "Macaulay, you were bold, brave, funny ... and very sexy."

Vogel experienced a rush of relief. "Thank you," he mumbled. "I ..."

"Mac, is everything alright, sugar?"

"Yes, of course." He shrugged, embarrassed. "It's just ..."

"You can tell me, *skattie*," she murmured, her tawny, cat-like eyes crinkling with concern. "After all, Tiger, I used to know all your secrets!"

"Y'know, you're just as ..." Vogel's eyes moistened with gratitude. "Grethe," he muttered thickly as he reached out. "Darling ..."

"Mac?" Grethe drew back sharply.

"Oh sorry, sorry ... God, I feel so stupid. Grethe, I didn't mean ..."

"Of course you did," she beamed at him. "But, Mac, I have a partner."

Vogel looked away helplessly. He was confounded. He didn't know where to place his offending hand. Grethe patted Vogel's flapping hand. "Tell me, Macaulay - did it hurt horribly when I broke off with you?"

There was a cheery ring tone, a familiar cartoon melody. Grethe reached for a tiny silver cell phone that the archivist had not noticed behind the salad bowl. "He what?" snapped Grethe into the receiver. "Sweetheart, I think you know - yes? - what you can tell Andries to do with himself." She flicked off the phone and moved her hand up to caress Vogel's cheek.

"Mac, we need to be sensitive, especially now. So I'd be very careful, darling, not to talk too much about things like, what was it ... black petals?"

For the first time the archivist noticed how Anglo-Saxon Grethe now sounded. It occurred to him that, all these years later, what most united their various former associates from the past, his male friends at least, was that they'd all - even Rafik - slept with Grethe.

He asked abruptly, "Do you remember Marc Hendricks?"

"Naturally, darling,' replied Grethe, glancing at her watch.

"I think I saw him. He seems to be leading that demonstration in Spin Street. They booed as I walked past, shouted insults at me." He shrugged. "I suspect it was Marc, actually, who was egging them on."

"Doesn't surprise me. Lenny says quite a few comrades have lapsed back into safe old patterns." She glanced at her watch again. "But our job, darling, is to work on ourselves. Our identity as, y'know, white Africans."

"I saw Rafik last week. He said we whites still had everything far too easy, even those who were in the struggle, and that's why so many whiteys are disillusioned. He said it's because we never really had to fight ..."

"Was it wise to discuss your file with Rafik?" interrupted Grethe.

"You know about my ...?"

"Word gets around, darling."

"Yes," said Vogel bitterly. "I should have known."

"We're all sorry about Marda, Mac, but you can't hide away in the past, precious." There was a sound of wheels crunching on gravel. They turned to see a black limousine with tinted windows turn into the driveway. Grethe leaned down and kissed Vogel wetly on the lips. "One nugget of advice, sweetheart. Move on, hm? Get a life, Mac. Destroy those files."

Eleven

WHEN Vogel got home there were two messages on his phone from Sivuyile.

"*Salam*, how's my *umlungu*? I need to see you right away. Besides, it's been too long. Time to catch up, friend! Don't delay. Call me, bru."

Sivuyile's second message, recorded two hours later, was equally succinct. "Hey, no call. What's with you white folk? Yho, speed it up, Mac."

The last time the archivist had seen Sivuyile Gqabe had been over three years before at Zechariah and Mary Xaba's home. They'd organised a small anniversary reunion, including Edwin and Rafik. Sivuyile had turned up with a gangly Afrikaans girl less than half his age: a runner-up, he announced proudly, in the previous year's Miss Western Cape beauty pageant. Sivuyile had been an important resistance lawyer in the Eastern Cape, the recipient of many 'black petal' messages from Vogel and Grethe. Later, after he had transferred to Cape Town and joined the local network of dissident lawyers, Sivuyile had at one time or another helped them all with free legal assistance over police harrassment and arbitrary detentions.

Hearing Sivuyile's voice stirred up disjointed feelings for Vogel. He was eager to ask his view on their shared past. The lawyer, after all, had introduced him to Marda. But what could - or should - he say about finding that dossier marked 'Sivuyile wakwa Gqabe' among the police files at the Castle? Vogel resolved not to answer the call immediately.

On Tuesday morning a playful wind sprung up, veering alternatively south-east to south-west, floating moisture in from the ocean, with blessed hints of rain from the gale out in the Atlantic, plus some slight relief from the heat over the city. That evening, however, when Vogel left the Castle, the wind was once again breathy and hot, and by Wednesday any skittish promise of rain had dried into a gritty desert sigh from the north.

Vogel fretted over Grethe's assertion that the term 'black petals' must have been his invention. That was not how he remembered it, at all. She was the creative one. At first they had merely cut hollows out of the centre of Bibles, and placed messages inside the secret compartment. Then it had been Grethe's idea to use actual verses from the Bible, re-arranging words from agreed chapters, so that if intercepted the content would only be intelligible to those who shared the code. "Like leaves falling from a tree," she'd explained, "making sense only to those who know where to look." He could still hear her excited exclamation, "black petals!" as one evening they were cutting out individual letters, words and phrases from a Bible.

At first he had chosen his own favourite passage, *The Epistle of Paul the Apostle to the Romans*, verse two, chapter two: "Therefore thou art inexcusable, O man, whosoever thou art that judgest: for wherein thou judgest another, thou condemnest thyself; for thou that judgest doest the same things." It amused Vogel to imagine a secret policeman reading this verse, not knowing that there was a hidden meaning therein. Later, he and Grethe developed a more precise sequence, so that the recipient of any communication would know exactly where to look in the Bible, finding the authorised text for that day according to the liturgical calendar.

After that, when Grethe had become a courier herself, they'd branched out even further - creating original word sequences, with titles, that Grethe could pass off as her own abstruse poems. These, definitely, they'd referred to, always, as their "black petals."

Vogel proceeded through the files systematically, logging and classifying every one, as well as creating a register of names mentioned in each dossier so that they could be cross-referenced and checked. It was tedious and routine work. As he did so, he kept worrying about Grethe's apparent forgetfulness. Had she actually not remembered, or did she prefer not to be reminded - or was it, in fact, his own memory which was at fault?

76

Early in the afternoon on Wednesday, as heat overwhelmed his tiny office, Vogel heard a floorboard squeak behind him. He turned to find a soldier in crisp green fatigues lounging against the inside of the open doorway, cigarette in hand, smiling.

"Must be fascinating work," grinned the soldier. "I've been watching you for ages." He stepped further into the room and held out a hand. "Hiya. Lieutenant Welcome Nxumalo."

The lieutenant peered round the cramped room, weakly lit by the single bare bulb. "Interesting. Like a prison. What can a white civilian, one wonders, be doing cooped up in here all day? Even our commander doesn't seem to know. Most peculiar. So us officers have staked big bets about you. General Dhlomo guessed that you're a spook of some kind." Lieutenant Nxumalo laughed. "Me, I guessed you're a forgotten military bureaucrat of the old regime - and that you spend your days locked away in here reading pornography."

The lieutenant casually picked up the dossier that Vogel had been working on. "Hmm, and what mysteries have we here?"

Vogel politely took the file out of his hand. "Sorry. It's private."

"Of course." The lieutenant grinned. "Well, looks like General Dhlomo wins the bet, eh?"

"I'm the only one allowed in this room," apologized the archivist, taking Lieutenant Nxumalo by the arm and guiding him back to the door.

Nxumalo lingered, half in the sunshine, trying to draw Vogel into conversation.

"They say this is the oldest building in South Africa," he remarked. "That's rubbish, of course. There're all sorts of structures up north, built hundreds of years before you whities arrived - stone walls, ruins of huge royal enclosures and so on. But they're African, so they don't count."

Vogel didn't respond. Nxumalo pointed to the grey stone bastion opposite. "That's where they used to execute prisoners. After drawing and quartering them, along with various other European delicacies, naturally."

Vogel supposed that the lieutenant had been sent to check up on him, to snoop: to spy. "Lieutenant, I've got quite a lot of work actually ..."

"Yes, I can see!" Lieutenant Nxumalo chuckled. "I'll drop by again, continue our fascinating chat." He turned to go. "Oh, by the way, Vogel ..."

Vogel wondered how he knew his name. He deliberately hadn't given it away.

"Me, I'd close up early today, you know," continued Nxumalo casually. "There's going to be a public demonstration this evening in the Grand Parade, against water restrictions. There'll be big crowds, probably thousands, angry as hell. Could get nasty." He grinned. "Tonight we're on emergency duty, so I guess they're thinking it might get violent."

"Thanks," said Vogel. To sound cordial, he added, *"Hamba kakuhle."*

The lieutenant waved. *"Ciao,"* he replied.

At home, there was a new, more urgent message from Sivuyile. There'd been one the previous evening, too. "Mac, quit pissing around," declared Sivuyile crisply. "I'm not kidding, man. I've made an appointment for you - tomorrow, my office, five. It'll be to your advantage, my friend. Trust me. Confirm with my secretary."

The Grand Parade was still strewn with litter from the previous evening's demonstration as Vogel, having locked his office early, hurried for his five o'clock appointment. Sivuyile's secretary had stressed the importance of punctuality. Vogel lingered at the corner of Spin Street in the doorway of a white and pink art deco building. The human cordon around the construction site had swelled considerably, blocking off all traffic. Protesters with placards had also gathered around the slave plaque on the pedestrian island, and from the centre of this throng, unmistakably, Vogel heard the rasping voice of Marc Hendricks leading a new chant.

"Slavery lives, slavery lives ..."

The archivist waited till he was sure no one had noticed him, then made a final dash down Corporation Street. Sivuyile's chambers were in a modern all-glass office block on the eleventh floor. The slender, sari-clad secretary, with whom he'd made the appointment, ushered Vogel into an empty oak-paneled board room.

"Mr. Gqabe is still in conference," she smiled. "He'll be with you shortly, sir. Would you care for tea or coffee?"

"Not really," replied Vogel. "A brandy, perhaps."

The only decoration on the dark paneling was an official photograph of the President and half a dozen oil portraits of elderly white businessmen. Along the length of the opposite wall extended a picture window with a panoramic view of Table Mountain. The colossal landmark was etched starkly against a clear cobalt sky and Vogel watched, absorbed, as the minute cable-car shivered up this craggy, unfeasibly imposing backdrop.

"At the booze already? That's the old Macaulay, the one we knew and loved!"

Vogel was startled. He'd expected to see Sivuyile in a svelte, three-piece charcoal grey suit, like the one in his picture in the foyer. Instead he wore a flowing indigo blue cotton robe. The lawyer threw open his arms to embrace Vogel in a breathless bear-hug.

"Welcome, comrade, to the palace of Mammon!"

Sivuyile released his grip. "Ah, I see you are admiring my outfit," he grinned. "Designed to impress a visiting group of investors from Germany."

"But it's West African," objected Vogel.

"Don't be a pedant, Mac. They don't know the difference. Please, it's a traditional costume. Africa, y'know - lions, elephants, natives, tom-toms."

Sivuyile's laugh was honeyed and contagious; it rumbled around the room, seeming to roll back from the oak-paneled walls. When Vogel had first met Sivuyile as a harassed young lawyer in Bisho, his colleagues had called him 'Sampson' because he was so poor and scrawny. Today Sivuyile Gqabe was imposing, noisy and confident.

"Congratulations, Sivu," began Vogel, "you certainly look ..."

"Prosperous?"

"No, fit."

"Gym, Mac. Three times a week. Weights, cycling, the whole damn crucifixion." Sivuyile winked. "Does miracles for your sex life, too."

He waved his hand. "Come, sit. Hell, there's too much to catch up on! How's Sarkissian?" Before Vogel could reply, the lawyer added, "And the evergreen, lovely Susan?"

His eyes glinted with amusement. Vogel couldn't tell if his friend was being mischievous. That booming humour had become part of his defenses. When a miserably paid attorney in the Eastern Cape, defending political detainees and persecuted himself, he had used, professionally, his European 'Christian' name: Enoch. Only in recent years had he developed sufficient assurance to revert to his given isiXhosa name, Sivuyile.

"And your work," continued Sivuyile. "Tell me about your work."

"What's this stuff?" asked Vogel, pointing to the other side of the teak boardroom table, where there was an array of film paraphernalia: a slim, flat screen, as well as an elaborate video camera on a tripod, attached to what appeared to be a generator and electronic equipment.

"White man's magic!"

"Looks like a film studio."

"Satellite link-up. Means that we can have a video conference with partners anywhere in the world - New York, Hong Kong, Sydney, London."

"Sivu, are you branching out into show-business?"

"Sure. I guess you could say what we do here is an off-shoot of the entertainment industry. Talking of which, Mac - tell me about your files."

"Files?" replied Vogel, startled, "Sivu, I don't know what ..."

"Don't bullshit me, comrade. Not after all we've been through."

"But how do you ..."

"The grapevine, Mac," Sivuyile guffawed, the echo reverberating round the sombre oak paneled boardroom. "Everything leaks. Secrets drip, confidences trickle. In the end, information always escapes. Hell, one can't keep anything quiet for long, especially in this town. Facts just ... seep out. You know that. It's what keeps us in business. I mean, you always say files leak, too - that they have a life of their own."

Vogel was bewildered. He didn't recall repeating anything like this to Sivuyile. In fact, he wasn't sure that in the past, at a time when he used to see the lawyer regularly, that he'd ever made jokes about the secret lives of documents. No, that was only something that he had dreamed up in recent years, as he examined a wider range of classified state archives.

"Sivu, those files are restricted. Strictly official secrets and all that."

"Obviously, and who understands better than me? I'm a lawyer, for heaven's sake. But, Mac, I gather you've been asking questions. That you've some doubts of your own."

Vogel hesitated. There was one uncertainty that Sivuyile would be able to resolve better than anyone. The lawyer was observing him with sardonic detachment.

"Macaulay," he said softly, "in the old days, when I acted for our guys in jail, usually I only got to see them after they'd been held in solitary and beaten up - and still they used to tell me stuff that could get them hung. You all trusted me, remember? Mac, relax. This isn't a police state any more."

"Okay," began Vogel anxiously. "But this is just between you an'..."

"And all the other people you've approached already!"

"You're right. Sorry."

Sivuyile leaned forward. "I hear you were asking about Marda."

"Did Susan Sarkissian tell you that?"

"What is it you need to know, Mac?"

"Or Grethe Cilliers?"

"You want to find out if all the others knew about you and Marda?" The lawyer spread his hands apologetically. "What can I tell you, brother? Everything leaks."

There was a rap at the door and the oval face of his youthful secretary appeared. In a stage whisper, she called, "Five minutes, Mr. Gqabe."

"Thank you, Sukki," replied Sivuyile without turning. He waited to hear the door close. "So, *quid pro quo*, old friend - you must've come across my security branch file?"

The archivist remembered the exhilaration he had first felt when, late in the evening, he'd turned up the folder marked 'Sivuyile wakwa Gqabe', and then his bitter frustration on discovering that there was nothing inside.

"No," said Vogel, without a flicker. "Not a hint that you had any record at all, I'm afraid. Drawn a complete blank there, unfortunately."

Sivuyile shrugged, ceding no indication whether he was disappointed or his ego dented by the implication that the security police may not have bothered to keep tabs on him. "Still, those files could prove a handy resource, Mac. Mustn't let that go to waste."

There was another knock at the door. Sivuyile glanced at his gold-link wristwatch. A skinny white youth entered, his yellow T-shirt and peroxide hair clashing with the gloomy sobriety of the paneled boardroom. "*Molo*, boss," he called out cheerily.

"Hiya Rik," replied the lawyer. "Cool outfit, man!"

He turned to Vogel with a grin. "Don't be fooled by his vile surfer scruff. This white boy's hot. He creates unbelievable video voodoo."

Sivuyile jumped to his feet. "Come, Mac, I want to show you something." He strode over to the broad picture window. The archivist followed. The stately mountain seemed to loom over them, filling the entire frame, epic and immediate. Sivuyile listened for a moment, then swore.

"All this damn glass and you can't even open it," he exclaimed. "I wanted you to hear those deluded fools demonstrating in Spin Street. You've seen them? It's pathetic, Mac, screaming about prehistoric bones. They're now marching round the slave plaque, like it's a bloody holy site - only it's the wrong spot. It was probably a fir tree under which slaves were auctioned, and that was almost certainly further over, in Church Square. Does this matter? No! Because, my brother, there's actually another game going on here."

"Two minutes," called Rik softly. Vogel turned to see him adjusting the video camera. The wide screen, already turned on, flickered with static.

"We've complied with every damn legal requirement," continued Sivuyile. "But is it enough that we promised a public consultation process? Nope. Or that we offer negotiations about where the bones should be buried and commemorated? No ... because that's not what they want. Frankly, if these guys were really interested in the slaves they'd allow scientific tests. No doubt about it, because part of the nightmare of slavery is the continuing anonymity. We know so little. But testing, that could shed light on where the slaves came from - if teeth were filed, for example, it would show the slaves were from West Africa. And it would also tell us much more about their diet, what

82

diseases they suffered, how old they were when they died."

"One minute, boss," called Rik.

"See, Mac, there's another game going on here, entirely."

"The crowds are certainly getting bigger," agreed Vogel. "I try to avoid going home past Spin Street now. They're incredibly angry."

"You're not kidding. There's no reasoning with these guys."

"I think I know who their leader is," said Vogel.

"Aha, so you've spotted him, too. He's out to make trouble, Mac."

"The crowd booed me once. I imagine Marc was behind that."

"Our old comrade is a very bitter man, my friend."

"Thirty seconds, boss," murmured Rik.

"Marc Hendricks is a headache," sighed Sivuyile, taking Vogel firmly by the elbow and guiding him back towards the boardroom table and the TV equipment. "That's where you come in, my friend. Your collection of files at the Castle could prove very handy indeed."

"The files?"

"Sure." Sivuyile chuckled. "There must be a file on Marc. Yes sir, I'd bet on that. Oh yeah, I'm damn sure our extremely efficient former security cops would've dug up the grubby low-down on Comrade Marc Hendricks!"

"Gentlemen," interrupted Rik urgently. "Take your places, please."

"He was always a ruthless opportunist," continued the lawyer softly, indicating that Vogel should resume his seat. "An unscrupulous little ..."

"Boss," Rik indicated the seat next to Sivuyile. "Better if your guest sat there."

"Would you mind moving closer, Mac?"

"Ten seconds," counted Rik.

"Yep," continued Sivuyile as they took their seats, "of course, you know Marc Hendrick's problem?" He lowered his voice. "He's a coloured. Most of them, however they disguise it, are just wannabe whites. Let's face it, they still don't know who the hell they are. That's why they've latched so desperately onto those pathetic slave bones and Marc bloody Hendricks. But then Marc's only ever had one real cause - Marc Hendricks! See, that's why I wouldn't be at all surprised if the little shit turned out to be an *impimpi*." He smiled at Vogel. "So, Mac - what've you got on Marc in the files?"

"Five to go, boss."

Vogel stared at Sivuyile, astonished. "You think Marc Hendricks was an informer?"

"Well, there's bound to be some dirt. Something to give us leverage."

"Three, two ..." counted Rik.

"But ... but, Sivu, there is no file on Marc Hendricks."

"Ready to go, boss."

"Pity," murmured the lawyer.

"Okay, you're on!"

The lawyer took a deep breath and stared straight into the camera.

Vogel watched astonished as the TV screen composed instantly into the round, close-up features of a fresh-faced, implausibly young executive in crisp blue and white striped shirt with a tasteful grey and mauve silk tie. In the background were shelves of leather-bound books.

"Hey, Chicago," yelled Sivuyile exuberantly.

"Morning, Cape Town," replied the young man with a calm, mid-western lilt.

"It's evening here, Mr. Deacon," Sivuyile reminded him tactfully.

"Of course, and it's your fall while we're going into spring," smiled his respondent in Chicago affably. "Mind if I drink my cappuccino? I'll never get used to these differences."

The archivist, overwhelmed by surprise, found it hard to concentrate on their conversation. At one point he heard the man in Chicago ask Sivuyile to repeat his surname and the lawyer obliged, making a loud implosion with his tongue, like a cork popping on the "q" of Gqabe.

The enthusiastic face on the screen dissolved into laughter.

"That's Zulu, right?"

"Something like that, Mr. Deacon."

"And what does it mean, in your language?'

"Well," smiled the lawyer, "my first name, Sivuyile, means 'we are happy.'" Sivuyile twisted towards Vogel, so that his back was to the camera, and winked. "Mr. Deacon, that's exactly what we're going to do for you here, in Cape Town. Trust me, we're going to make you very happy, too."

"Great, Enoch. Tell me some good news about those religious nuts."

"Mr. Deacon, I'm very happy to inform you that I have with me here this evening the man who can unblock this whole confusion." Sivuyile turned with a theatrical wave and Vogel was aware of the camera swiveling to follow his gesture and of a lens pointing directly at him. "This is my old friend and trusted colleague, Dr. Macaulay Vogel."

"It's an honour, Dr. Vogel," said the man from Chicago solemnly.

"Dr. Vogel is extremely distinguished, Mr. Deacon. In fact, I must tell you - he is a hero of our struggle for liberation." Sivuyile had also, abruptly, become sombre. "Yes, he is, in addition, an acquaintance of Marc Hendricks, the ring-leader of these protesters, and Dr. Vogel has very kindly offered to play the role of *amicus curiae* ... and, even better, to act as an intermediary."

There was a hush as Vogel stared into the camera, not knowing what to say. The silence was broken by the voice across the Atlantic. "Dr. Vogel, I trust our friend Enoch has informed you that there'll obviously be a generous facilitation fee?"

"Justin, it's all taken care of," replied Sivuyile smoothly.

"Great, I guess that wraps up our conference."

"Construction will start any day, Justin, pretty much on schedule."

"Terrific. Then I'll sign off, Enoch. Have a good day, Cape Town."

"*Sala kahuhle*, Chicago!"

The screen went blank and Rik began dismantling his equipment.

"Marvelous," announced Sivuyile. "That went well, didn't it?"

"Sivu," said Vogel, flushed and angry. "You told ..."

The lawyer held up his hand. "Shh, not in front of the servants." He winked at Rik. "Another brandy, Dr. Vogel?"

They waited till the technician had packed up his equipment and left.

Vogel said heatedly, "You told him I was a hero of the struggle."

"But, Mac, you were. You are! If it was up to me, old friend, you'd have a chest full of medals - the order of this, honour of that."

"You also told him that I would act as an intermediary with Marc Hendricks."

"Macaulay, what is it that you really want? Looking up past comrades, asking weird questions, raking up old stuff? What, actually, are you after?"

"I just want to understand … where I stand. Going through the files has unraveled things. I'm confused about the past, myself." The archivist's breathing was rapid and shallow. He sucked in air deeply. "I'm no longer sure what sort of a person I was, once."

Sivuyile shrugged. "You seem the same to me, comrade."

"I do?"

"Yeah, you're still a terrier. But maybe you should speak to Boschard."

"Colonel Boschard?" gasped Vogel. "Christ, Sivu, the last I heard you were intent on prosecuting the bastard, making him pay for his unspeakable crimes, the torture of our comrades …"

"No, you see, that's precisely why we can control him. Boschard's on our side now. Anyway, he's not actually the crude ogre that we used to imagine. He's smart, plays chess, reads poetry." Sivuyile chuckled, "The other day Boschard was quoting surreal Spanish verses at me. Federico García Lorca, for God's sake, who was shot by Franco's fascists!"

"Boschard's a …" Suddenly Vogel stopped. "Sivu, don't tell me you employ Colonel Boschard to do your dirty work these days?"

The lawyer shrugged. "All I'm saying, Mac, is that Boschard would have the answer to many of your questions."

"I'd rather have my tongue ripped out that sup with that butcher," hissed Vogel. "Forgive? Forget? Never! No, that's not what I want."

"Then what do you want?" interrupted the lawyer crisply. "What is it, precisely, that you need, Mac?"

"The files are a mess. They don't tally up. You just can't check or compare. I want - I need - to know if there are any other records, ones that they are not allowing me to see."

"Ah!" The lawyer chuckled, delighted. "We have the same problem."

"Oh, I hardly think there's any connection between police files and slave bones."

"Sensitivity, that's the problem. These are delicate times, Macaulay. People misunderstand too easily. Tensions are rising. The fire - well, was it arson or not? Then those cursed bones, and today another bomb."

He grinned, and for the first time Vogel noticed a diamond stud on a front tooth. "One can't go about things too directly. That's where I come in, comrade. Fact is, I have what they call 'connectivity.' *Quid pro quo ...*"

Sivuyile paused and beamed, his face iridescent. "You approach Marc Hendricks, act as go-between, and I'll extend my antenna into all the right places. See, that's the way to do it, Mac. Don't blunder around. No, *Bhuti*. Put out feelers." He winked. "Let 'em come to you."

Sivuyile roared with laughter. "Works with women, anyway ..."

Twelve

VOGEL wrote a brief letter to Marc Hendricks. Or rather, he wrote to Marc's wife Zeena. He could, he knew, have simply walked down to Spin Street and delivered the message in person.

That weekend trudged by, the lingering hours progressively more oppressive. The only occasion the archivist left his house was to post the letter. The sky was ashen, emitting a milky glare. As he strode back from the post office on Saturday morning, gasps of uneven wind flipped litter and plastic bags onto security spikes and razor-wire. Vogel noticed how walls in his neighbourhood were creeping higher and becoming more fortified.

He passed by a café in Dunkley Square. Despite the blanched midday glare, candles lit each table inside and he heard a waft of careless laughter. No one was out in the scratchy, wind-scoured streets. Even the gaudy pastels of Sabata Dalindyebo Way seemed subdued and diffident in this cruel and monochrome light.

He felt restless, ill-at-ease. He had accepted Sivuyile's invitation. It was now a matter of waiting. His phone rang twice and both times Vogel rushed to listen to the message; each time it was Zechariah Xaba, expressing concern and urging him to call back.

The archivist felt trapped, powerless. The files had thrown up one morsel, and then - as if they had a spiteful resolve of their own - cruelly clammed up. He was sure he had exhausted his search among the records stored at the Castle. Now any resolution to his dilemma appeared to be out of his control. He was dependent on others to provide him with the evidence that he sought. It was the waiting that made him fidgety. As long as he was examining archives Vogel felt that he retained some control. Clarification depended on his patience, cunning and skill. But it was as if these archives were a sly, breathing opponent. Files, he reflected, did not just have a life of their own; like a stubborn antagonist, they seemed to posses a capricious humour all their own - what was given with one hand, was taken away with another. For the moment, Vogel knew the documents had outwitted him.

The thought of his own dossier in the drawer upstairs began to weigh him down. He felt its malign presence. He couldn't stop brooding over it. The fact that a police file containing details about his own past movements and associations was locked away in his study upstairs haunted his thoughts, increasingly upsetting him as the weekend dragged on. The contents seemed to seep out and fill the entire house with their malevolent spirit.

He had taken the file on a whim, entirely contrary to his professional ethics and cautious nature. That decision taunted him, as did the existence of the file in his home. Its toxic exhalations oozed after him, as though there were an injured, winded beast upstairs. These infected thoughts followed him everywhere, even when he tried to distract them by watching television.

A degraded, oppressive irritability fouled the house. He busied himself cleaning and scrubbing, attempting to cleanse this unshakable mood of impurity. Vogel swept and hoovered, clearing away eddies of bougainvillea petals which had turned crusty and transparent with time. But he could not expunge or escape the spreading, venomous discharge from his hidden file, which seemed to corrupt the air in every room.

It was with relief that Vogel returned to work at the Castle on Monday. He busied himself with routine. As always, he found distraction in following a rigorous procedure. In the initial frantic search for his 'personal' file the archivist had actually disrupted the order that at the outset of this assignment he had started to impose on these documents. Once again he took up the task of rearranging the files in systematic categories: alphabetical, chronological, geographic, numerical and occupational - hunter or hunted.

Vogel began to compile lists of case reference numbers to see if there was a pattern. Most had no alphabetical prefix. In the case of his own dossier, he deduced that CCT indicated that he had lived and operated in central Cape Town. Others appeared to refer to an individual's geographical base: PE for Port Elizabeth, or KWT for King William's Town. Files from police headquarters in Pretoria added a racial index: SI, S2, S3 and S4 to indicate whether the suspect was white, Indian, Coloured or black. There were also codes for agents and informers. MI, he felt certain, referred to Military Intelligence, while he knew that the designation RS indicated a police spy.

By midday he had regained his composure, feeling that he still preserved some degree of control.

On his way home Vogel stopped at the flower market and bought a hefty bouquet of blue irises. In Adderley Street, waiting at the traffic lights opposite the Slave Lodge, he heard the by now expected chant from Spin Street: "Slavery lives, Slavery lives." As the archivist stood before his front door in Sabata Dalindyebo Way, the telephone rang. Hurriedly he unlocked the door, placed the bouquet by the picture of Marda and ran to answer the phone. He was convinced it would be either Sivuyile or Marc Hendricks.

"Macaulay," exclaimed Zechariah Xaba. "We were getting worried, *Bhuti*. Mary was upset. Very. She was even thinking you could've been run over or drowned. What's up, man, that you don't return our calls anymore?"

Zechariah brushed aside Vogel's protestations that he'd been too busy. In the absence of Michael, Zechariah had acted like an older brother - and although Zech was only seven years older, since his marriage to Mary he'd also begun to act more like a father. Zech's rumbling, baritone preacher's voice was comforting, even cheering, and for Vogel it was with a burst of pent up, exhilarating relief that he finally confessed to Zechariah about the call from Deputy Minister Biyela. He described the disordered collection of documents that had been dumped in the room at the Castle and how he had, shockingly, discovered his own file. Vogel admitted that, against regulations, he had taken this dossier home and confided that the presence of this file now tormented him, polluting his home and poisoning his thoughts.

"Okay," said Zechariah calmly. "Was there anything compromising? Anything ... horribly personal. Something you might be ashamed of?"

"My God, no - nothing like that. No, there's just things there I don't remember. Information, details, stuff about me that seems like someone else. It's not me. I really don't recognise this person, Zech. I'm confused."

Zechariah was relaxed, reassuring. "The first thing to do, Macaulay, is to get that file out of your house," he said. "Normally, as you know, I hate this secrecy … the way our guys, as soon as they're in authority, also love mysteries, wanting to keep everything under wraps. All these documents should be made public, flushed out into the light of day. But you're in a fix, Mac. So take the damn thing back - first thing tomorrow morning."

"You're right," replied Vogel, relieved. "Of course, that's it. Thanks, yeah … take the dossier back. Absolutely, end of story. File it. Forget it."

"That's my boy. No more secrets. Promise?"

"Totally. The whole thing's just been building up. Crazy, isn't it? I mean, all those worries, all that uncertainty was mostly a panicky figment of my imagination. I should've told you before, Zech. I feel better already."

"Excellent. But there is one other thing, Macaulay. This is a must. Lunch, here, Saturday, at the usual time. Hm? Mary won't take no for an answer, y'know. Promise?"

The following morning Vogel stuffed the lime green folder into a dufflel bag and set out for work in high spirits. Salty flurries of wind braced off the Atlantic.

The stone walls of the Castle gleamed in the sunlight, and Vogel greeted the duty guard cheerfully. As he headed towards his office, Vogel noticed that there were more seagulls than tourists in the courtyard.

He unlocked the scruffy timber door to his office and switched on the light. Under the weak glow of the single bulb, the files were stacked high and mute, just as he had left them on Friday. The archivist almost expected one day to catch a final flurry of furtive movement as a last guilty document scuffled back into place after a nighttime of secretive re-arrangement. Vogel smiled to himself at the absurdity of this nightmare. The files were static, indifferent … lifeless, and as he scrutinised the overcrowded room it seemed to Vogel that, for the first time in weeks, these documents were at last returning to their inevitable, designated order and discipline, and he felt a glow of pleasure and reassurance.

Vogel locked the door and removed the lime green folder from his duffel bag. An immediate and exhilarating swell of confidence flushed through Vogel as he considered the stacks of files that he had begun to regroup. There was no question where his own file should be slotted in: alphabetically, under "V", and in the section for the Western Cape.

There were perhaps only fifty or so other dossiers in that category, U to X, and Vogel rapidly flicked past the first seven files until he came to V. There was a Van Vuuren, a Vraagom and a Visser. He was about to place the faded green folder in his hand into the stack when he saw that the dossier underneath was clearly marked: 'Vogel, Macaulay, personal.'

At first the archivist felt a stab of fury. He had been hunting for this desperately, moving documents uselessly from one side of the room to the other. How had he missed it? It could, of course, have been sheer exhaustion or the initial frenzied, disordered nature of his search. Perhaps he'd picked up two files at once, by accident, or maybe he had actually seen this but, subconsciously, not really wanted to find it.

He picked up the stained beige folder. It was quite substantial.

Stamped on the front was his personal reference number: CCT10/36.

Vogel was struck by a sudden suspicion: what if someone had been tampering with the files in his absence? He thought of the smiling Lieutenant Nxumalo. And yet the files appeared to be exactly as he'd left them when he had locked the office on Friday.

He opened the folder. There were scores of sheets of lined official paper inside. He took out the first page. His eye was instantly drawn to a name, typed: Mrs. Sarkissian. He wondered why Susan should be mentioned in an old security police report. Susan had never been involved in their activities, and had only come onto the scene later, just at the point when everything was changing. He looked at the date at the top of the page. Then, with a nauseating lurch, Vogel realized that this did not refer to Susan.

He never thought of Marda as Mrs. Sarkissian. He read the words on the page. They were his words, Marda's words. He remembered the time, exactly. They had been talking on the telephone; hurried, secretive, frantic to arrange a time to meet. His anxiety, his longing was palpable in every word.

Someone had been listening; the line must have been bugged. It was an exact transcription. He could hear Marda's voice. He could tell when she laughed or teased, and felt again the yearning that filled their silences: all the small, important private things that an eavesdropping policeman would have misconstrued and which had been blanked out in this pitiless, typed facsimile. Sometimes Marda was even referred to only by her case reference code: MB33.

Vogel sat down. He took out the lined sheets one by one. There was a thesaurus of information. How busy they must have been. There were other names, particulars, dates and times. He barely noticed. Most reports detailed assignations with Marda: time, place, duration ... his home, her car, a café. Some contained a summary of their conversations while others recorded the complete exchange; her endearments, covetous quarrels, and his desperation.

Vogel sat at the bare wooden table under the single feeble bulb and those words scattered over him like a burst of cloying black petals, each one deliquescing instantly, eviscerating his heart, for he could hear every remark as if Marda was beside him in the stuffy room - those sealed years since her death expunged as he felt, again, that tender rasp and taste of her supple skin, the warm scents of her body, the ripe astringency of her lemony perfumes. Half-choked sobs heaved out of his throat, and for the first time in nearly twenty-five years the archivist surrendered entirely to his overpowering loss.

Every word, clichéd endearment, each innocent phrase or ardent exchange was so intensely personal that Vogel wondered how any human being could bear or dare to eavesdrop. Yet his most intimate moments were clinically annotated, impersonally recorded, as if observed by an unruffled, God-like spectator. He felt defiled. It was unbearable, as though a nameless deity had delved deep into his body and dabbled, with hygienically-gloved fingers, into the throbbing recesses of his exposed soul. Vogel felt betrayed.

A barrier had broken; the restraining dyke of language had finally been breached, unleashing a tornado of disorder and malevolent chaos. He could barely see the typed words on the page. Vogel couldn't keep the individual letters in focus. They seemed to slither and scatter.

Waxy tears trickled onto the reports.

The archivist picked up further sheets of typed A4 paper and stared uncomprehending as familiar words slipped hopelessly away from sense and meaning. He was holding up another page when, out of a cluster of more jumbled words, a list of names, bunched together, struck him forcefully: Gershon, Malek, Isak, Nadira. Vogel closed his eyes and breathed in deeply. His heart thumped violently. All but the last one were names that he hadn't mentioned for over forty years - barely even remembered - yet they were as present and startling to him as if someone had violently battered down the office door.

Vogel looked at the top of the page, willing himself to concentrate. The capital letters, in slightly smudged type, said, 'Family history.' It was all there, encapsulated in one brief, red lined official-issue sheet of paper: father Gershon Vogel, mother Nadira (née October), and his brother Michael's real name, Malek. The information was terse, factual.

There was the name he had been registered with at birth, which was engraved on his birth certificate, but there was also the one that he had been known by during his first four years, the one that his mother and father had fought over so much. His father had wanted him to be called Isak, after his own grandfather. But Gershon had been away at sea at the time of the birth, so it was only a good deal later, by accident, that Gershon Vogel discovered that his wife had in fact officially baptized their second son as Macaulay.

Abruptly, seeing these names in cold print, he remembered the terrible arguments when he was a small boy, before his father finally abandoned them: his mother saying that even by just calling him 'Isak' people could tell that he wasn't European and his father shouting that they had no reason to be ashamed of who or what they were and that he would never teach his sons to pretend to be someone else, or identify themselves by other, false names.

He read this numbly, as if reading about someone else. It was all there, recorded in forensic, bureaucratic detail. That his father Gershon Vogel had left when he was four years old; that his mother then promptly removed them from the rural mission station to Cape Town, where no one knew them, and created a new, assumed life; that she had begun calling Malek, his older brother, 'Michael' and himself 'Macaulay'; that Nadira had got a job as a filing clerk in a 'whites only' hospital and sent them to white schools … and that, much later, his brother had left the country and never come back.

There were other things that Vogel didn't know. Gershon Vogel had re-married, he'd had another family. Vogel had always understood their father had died not long after abandoning them. He read about his father with no emotion. He thought dazedly, the cops must have spent weeks researching this. The report also mentioned his grandmother Ansiela who had lived out at the rural mission station a few hours east of Cape Town.

Vogel remembered traveling by bus from Cape Town to visit the old lady once a year until she died when he was nearly eight. Thereafter he and Michael lived a secluded life with their mother in Yonge Street. She had protected them by never mentioning their past. A security policeman had evidently been out to the mission station, for someone had meticulously copied out a birth register and concluded, "It is possible to trace the maternal side back four generations. The suspect's great-great grandmother was the freed slave, Catharina van Petronella (no other recorded name)."

The archivist read this with detached curiosity. The tornado of emotion that had assaulted him earlier had subsided. It was like studying the file of someone else entirely. He had simply, conveniently, blanked out his early childhood, the first four years before they moved to Cape Town. He felt disconnected. Vogel placed the sheets of paper back into the beige folder.

He looked at his watch: it was half past ten. He picked up the lime green folder that he'd brought back from home that morning and had intended to return, and carefully tucked both dossiers into his duffel bag.

Outside the breeze was gusting strongly, chasing in scuds of cloud from the sea. Vogel locked the door and walked swiftly along the ramparts. At the Katzenellenbogen bastion a solider sheltering from the wind lounged against the protective northern wall, smoking. As Vogel hurried down the steps, Lieutenant Nxumalo raised a hand in ironic salutation.

Wind blustered in restless flurries across the Grand Parade. In the flower market he bought a dozen pink and ivory white lilies, the delicate trumpet-shaped *Amaryllis belladonna*. Even though it was only mid-morning, the archivist automatically followed his habitual evening route home down Adderley Street. He felt numb. Why had the security police never used any of the information they had so assiduously gathered on him?

As he waited to cross the road, opposite the Slave Lodge, he heard the muffled chant from Spin Street, "Slavery lives, Slavery lives ..."

He strode down Government Avenue. Oak trees sighed, leaves skittered. Vogel had walked through the public gardens down this narrow lane all his working life. It felt as if he was being marched back into the past.

The wrap of cloud on the summit of Table Mountain had turned darker and rivulets of vapour gushed over the edge, dissolving in the warmer air below like a suspended waterfall. Vogel lingered for a moment to stare at the gaudy colours in Sabata Dalindyebo Way. It was as if the past had been painted over. When a boy, the houses had all been crumbling, with peeling paint. But his mother had been absurdly proud of Yonge Street. "Sir George Yonge was sent here as Governor," Nadira used to remind him and Michael, "because of his great friendship and influence with King George III."

Nadira also named him after the nineteenth century British historian. "Macaulay, not Isak, is you who are," she'd insist fiercely. "Be proud of it!"

He unlocked his front door. It was dark inside. He didn't turn on the light. Vogel laid his garland on the wooden sideboard before the photograph. He stared at the portrait of Marda and wondered if he had in fact told her. Probably not. As he'd grown up, others simply assumed he was white and Vogel had allowed their acceptance. Whiteness, he discovered, was a state of grace: paradoxically, it made him both invisible and a someone.

Had he lied to anyone? No. To Marda? No! It was an unimportant detail; that was not who he was. It didn't define him. Then there came a moment when too much time had lapsed for him to easily and plausibly, or honourably, set the record straight and reclaim that part of himself which his mother had so successfully buried. It would be embarrassing now to tell any of his friends. The time when he could reasonably have revealed his secret had passed. It would be awkward, false; too uncomfortable for everyone.

When had this happened? He didn't know. The moment had somehow slipped by. He was trapped: whiteness had become his identity.

Vogel hurried upstairs and locked both folders, green and beige, into his study drawer.

Thirteen

THE following morning Vogel set out for work, as was his habit, at seven forty-five. The sky was pearly and wind ricocheted down Sabata Dalindyebo Way in forceful gasps. There were only a couple of other people in Government Avenue, also hurrying to work, wrapped up and heads down. As he reached Wale Street a hasty squall funneled down Adderley Street nearly toppled him over. Vogel felt its humid, briny lick.

The thought of proceeding down Adderley Street and hearing the mournful chant about slave bones repelled him. He turned left and began a directionless wander through the wind-emptied streets of the city centre, drifting further westward, away from the Castle and unforgiving files.

Vogel crossed into the pedestrian St. George's Mall, circled aimlessly round the cobbles of Greenmarket Square, veered south up Long Street, battled against the wind down Loop, right again up Bree, back down Buitgengracht, hardly noticing where he walked, except that among the few out in the open he observed several well-wrapped women disappear into doorways or turn street corners and each time his spirits soared as for one euphoric instant he imagined he had seen the vanishing silhouette of Marda.

As a car passed he glimpsed her in the back of the head of a female passenger; he saw her in a dark-coated woman who rushed, head down, into Hout Street. He saw Marda through the windows of cafés as he circled the deserted flea-market in Greenmarket Square once more. He saw her in the casual toss of a head, the gloss of someone's hair, the gesture of a woman's hand, and as he lingered in the doorway of one café he even heard Marda in the cadence of women's voices or soft laughter. She was everywhere.

The archivist walked aimlessly. He saw Marda in slim women, plump women, fair women, dark women. Something bizarre Rafik had said on their last meeting surfaced in his mind: "Marda means 'giant' in Arabic."

Vogel kept trudging until his feet ached and his face was chafed from the remorseless wind and still he could not smother the pain. These were the familiar streets that he had walked and loved all his life, and yet now he felt he hardly recognized them: Loop, Long, Dorp, Strand, Waterkant. Even the names suddenly seemed outlandish and alien to him.

"You white people," Rafik had declared, finally breaking the strained silence as he held the front door open to banish Vogel from his home, "you always suspect the worse of us. But you know something, Macaulay? If you have suspicions, you must look closer to home."

A salty blast pummeled him across the open expanse of Riebeeck Square. On the other side of the car park was the fenced-off St. Stephen's Church. Vogel thought of how, every time they'd passed, his mother had proudly reminded him and Michael that it had been built by Sir George Yonge, as the first theatre in Cape Town, for British troops stationed here during the Napoleonic Wars. Half a century later the building had been stoned by a white mob, enraged that it was being used for a Sunday service for freed slaves. The building was re-named after Stephen, the first Christian martyr - stoned to death while Saul of Tarsus held the clothes of the mob.

"Hey, bossie - you want I lookout your car?"

He turned. A crumpled, liver-coloured woman lurched towards him. "No one steals your car when Dulcie's here, boss. S'true, everyone knows Dulcie. No one messes with me." She waved at two other vagrants lying under the gum tree. "Don't talk to these *skollies*, sir. Ttsst, they drunk." She winked. "No, you be nice with Dulcie. Dulcie is your only girlfriend, hey?"

Vogel protested he was on foot, but the woman followed him. "Don't talk to no other girls, you hear? Dulcie will lookout that car, no problem."

Vogel increased his pace and behind him he heard the woman yell, "Ooh but my master's so white 'n fine Dulcie could drink him down!"

As he hurried away the archivist thought of Rafik's final barb before he'd slammed the door. "You white people," he had shouted bitterly, "you understand nothing. Even now, you just fly through life on a magic carpet."

He was not who people thought he was. Would it, Vogel wondered, have made any difference if he'd confessed to Rafik ... or, if he had called back to Dulcie, "My name is Isak. I am not who you think I am." People could still pretty much tell what shade your pigment was, without even seeing or hearing you, by knowing your name. To them, he was just another white man and no matter what anyone said pigment still counted.

Even now when he traveled a few hours out of Cape Town Vogel was repeatedly shocked to discover in isolated valleys that there were still farm labourers who lived as though they were marooned in the eighteenth century. Men had rocketed to the moon decades ago; yet in those remote valleys he always found the same downcast eyes and obsequious, servile manner - even to him, who'd risked so much that they could be free. All the labourers saw, however, was the illusion of his skin and the invisible armour of confidence with which it clothed him. Farm workers frequently lived in two-roomed hovels with no electric light, running water, sanitation or even, it seemed to Vogel, self-respect. Employers still regularly treated them - worse, they also seemed to feel themselves to be - like slaves. To them, too, Vogel appeared to be just another white man, swathed in the immunity of his colour.

Maybe Rafik was right: his pigment still cast a bewitching spell.

Vogel had been shocked to learn from the file that his grandmother Ansiela had lived at the mission station in Zoar. The previous summer, while Sarkissian had been absent in Johannesburg, he and Susan had driven out of Cape Town for the weekend and they were on a country road when he'd spotted a sign to Amalienstein, a former mission station. Without telling Susan why, he'd pulled off to tour Amalienstein in the belief that this was where once he used to visit his grandmother. Vogel had so comprehensively wiped his past from his own mind that he had forgotten that Ansiela had in fact lived in Zoar, the rival mission station only a few kilometers further on.

He wasn't who people thought he was. Who then? He no longer knew himself.

It was late afternoon before Vogel finally returned, exhausted, to Sabata Dalindyebo Way. His mind was at last numbed by the remorseless tramping of city streets and debilitating wind. He threw himself onto his bed, done in, and it was only when the phone rang some hours later that Vogel woke. For a moment he lay in the dark, listening to a woman's voice leaving a message on the answer phone. Then he leapt up and rushed to answer the call.

"Susan, I so glad you …"

"I'm only calling about Sarkissian," she interrupted. "He's still hoping, you know, that you'll call, Macaulay."

"Of course, if that's what you …"

"He wants to continue your mountain jaunts - just the two of you, without Rafik."

"Susan, we must talk."

"I've told Edwin you're busy. I don't want you seeing him anymore."

"Susie, I need to see you, urgently."

"I'm only telling you this in case he calls. Say you're too busy."

"Please? I feel terrible about … you know. Can't we meet, Susan?'

"No, I won't have Edwin hurt again, Macaulay. Stay away."

She hung up. Vogel had barely reached the door to turn on the light when the phone rang again. He turned back and picked up the receiver.

"Susie?"

"This is Zeena Hendricks, Mr. Vogel." She spoke in staccato bursts, as if she had rehearsed her message and it was distasteful or possibly contagious to speak to him. "My husband can see you at ten o'clock tomorrow. He will give you half an hour. My husband is a busy man, Mr. Vogel. Please be punctual." She rattled off an address in Athlone.

"Could you give me any other directions?" asked Vogel.

"Mr. Vogel, Athlone is not a foreign country." For the first time the archivist thought he could detect a tinge of humour in her voice. "Just follow the *bruin mense*."

Vogel found it difficult to sleep that night. The wind howled. It raged with a fury that had once sunk entire fleets of the Dutch East

India Company. Vogel had never become accustomed to the convulsive force of such winds, which frequently sounded as though they might rip the roof right off. The gale had eased by morning, but when he stepped into the street Vogel saw that the cloud massed over Table Mountain had huffed up sulkily.

Dust and litter swirled down the blanched streets. Flurries of wind pummeled his car. Eastward, along Kromboom, he noticed most drivers were no longer white, and when Vogel turned into Birdwood - as if he had crossed an invisible frontier - the few people out in the streets were Zeena Hendricks' *bruin mense*. He passed tufty grass verges, low concrete fences and newly painted bungalows. Vogel was surprised to discover that Marc Hendricks' street was more dilapidated than those nearby.

On the corner stood the pink, double storey pebble-dash of the New Apostolic Church; opposite languished a faded pistachio green bungalow with a broken iron gate. Marc Hendricks' house was smarter. A TV satellite dish spouted from the steep, chalet-style slate roof.

"I can see what you thinking, man, like it's a bubble coming out of your head," boomed Marc Hendricks, opening his front door. "Yeah, I saw you checking out the street an' *sommer* scheming, 'Why doesn't Marc Hendricks move into a smart white suburb, like all the other leaders?'"

He gestured Vogel to a fluffy, oversized armchair. In the next room the archivist could see a flickering TV screen. Zeena Hendricks hovered in the corridor, observing him. A fleecy white dog raced between her legs and began snapping at Vogel's ankles.

Hendricks remarked briskly, "I have a meeting in half an hour. Zeena, won't you ask Miriam to bring us some refreshments s'long?"

Vogel wondered why it had taken him so long to identify this rasping voice. It had deepened, but still possessed an uneasy, scratchy quality, as though his throat was so worn it might give way by the end of the sentence. This was what made Marc Hendricks such a thrilling, unpredictable orator. He had the fervour of a revivalist preacher, and Vogel remembered how the worry whether his croaky voice would hold out, added to the tension that at any moment he might say something risky or incredibly inflammatory kept listeners hovering between alarm and ecstasy. Marc Hendricks had been able to hold an audience of thousands in this state of rising expectation, even - perhaps especially - when surrounded by armed police or soldiers.

It had been a joke among their group that the voice should really have belonged to Zeena, for she was sturdy and powerfully built, whereas her husband had been skinny, positively scrawny, so that with his light russet complexion he would scarcely, otherwise, have been noticed on the streets of Cape Town. He had filled out a little, and now wore gold-rimmed glasses. The moment he opened his mouth, however, the room was filled with a saw-toothed energy. Although they were indoors Marc Hendricks wore his trade-mark baggy leather jacket, as if he were waiting for the call to action.

"What a sign of our times, eh?" Marc Hendricks shook his head. "That you, you of all people, should also marvel that I could still reside among my people." Vogel noticed several front teeth had gold fillings, which lent added fascination to the mesmerizing effect of watching that restless mouth. "But, Macaulay - how else, hm, would Moses have led the Israelites unless he too had remained faithfully amongst his own people?"

Vogel recalled the ornate language and how, even in the past, Marc Hendricks had seemed more comfortable talking to a crowd than to an individual. Back then he'd relied heavily on Zeena to negotiate social situations, and some even snidely whispered that while Marc had the energy and the tongue, it was Zeena who had the ideas and ambition.

"Yes, my friend, I have been bequeathed that historic mission, to lead my people to the Promised Land." Marc threw his arms wide to indicate the street outside, and possibly the entire city beyond. "You are surprised, my friend. No, don't deny it. I see it written upon your face, Macaulay."

He paused as though waiting for a reply, blazing eyes fixed on Vogel. The archivist shifted uncomfortably, but before he could reply Marc sighed, "Truly comrade, we overthrew one racial tyranny only to impose another."

Zeena entered, followed by their maid in dappled pink and green pinafore. She was an angular, awkward young black woman, wearing fluffy slippers and carrying a plastic tray warily.

"Miriam," instructed Zeena, "guests first, remember."

There was silence as the maid self-consciously handed Vogel a mug of instant coffee and rusks. "*Enkosi, sisi*," he murmured.

"First the white folk were on top, now it's the black," continued Marc, accepting a coffee cup without shifting his gaze from Vogel. "But ..."

"Thank you, Miriam," said Zeena sharply.

"What about the *bruin mense*, eh? What happened to them, comrade?"

Zeena replied. "We weren't white enough before," she said bitterly. "No, sir - and now we're not black enough."

"And that, old comrade in arms, is why I am a brown nationalist!"

Not long ago, Vogel remembered, Marc Hendricks had proudly, and in all his public orations, called himself 'black.' In those days, he had always pointedly insisted that a white speaker also share the limelight in order to openly demonstrate that their uprising was colourless. Although his wife was noticeably more socially adept, many of their white comrades had suspected - but never said so openly - that Zeena Hendricks despised white people.

"It is a fact, Macaulay. We are the floating people, uh-huh ... the in-between people, the 'not white' and the 'not black' people. Admit it, we are the 'who the hell are you?' people. Verily, even now, we are nothing people. Today, and God be my witness, we are still the forgotten people."

The archivist listened, mesmerized and uneasy. He sneaked a glance at his watch. Twenty minutes of his audience had already evaporated and he could see no way to politely interrupt his host.

"The white people, if I may speak freely, Macaulay, stole everything from us. Yes, they robbed us, not only of our liberty and dignity, they even thieved our language. Mm-hm, that is a fact, comrade. The slaves, our ancestors, first spoke Afrikaans - and what did the Dutch people do?"

He paused and Zeena answered for him. "They stole our language."

"That's right. Then what did those same white folk call themselves?"

"Afrikaners," murmured Zeena, staring accusingly at Vogel.

"But who, in the eyes of God, has the right to that name?"

"The *bruin mense*," replied Zeena, louder.

"Of course!" shouted Marc Hendricks. "We are the true Afrikaners. Rightfully, because we are both black and white. Truthfully, we, not *wit mense*, are the real Afrikaners." He glared at the seated archivist. "The fact is, my friend, the white people stole our identity."

"They stole it," echoed Zeena.

"So," Marc Hendricks lowered his voice. "Do you know what my mission is, Macaulay?"

The archivist looked uneasily from husband to wife.

"Now blacks are behaving exactly like the whites, imitating them. They're aggressive, arrogant, lording it over us, looking down on us. But who do these *moegoes* think they are?" Marc Hendricks glowered. "See, comrade? My calling is to take back what was stolen." He pointed at Vogel. "My mission ... our mission, my friend, is to seize back our identity."

"That's right," Zeena confirmed fiercely. "To take back what is ours."

In the next room Vogel heard the gasping inhalations of a hoover. He slid his eyes down to his watch again. His time was running out.

Tentatively he said, "And that, I suppose, is the point of the bones?"

"Cape Town is built on slave bones," snapped Zeena.

Vogel was taken aback by her ferocity. He was about to reply when she turned to her husband. "Let's wrap this up, Marc."

Marc Hendricks moved over to look out of the window. For the first time Vogel noticed that a dark blue saloon car had parked in their narrow driveway. Two sturdy men in charcoal grey suits now stood beside it. Seeing Hendricks at the window, they saluted in unison.

"Quit beating about the bush, Macaulay." Marc Hendricks glanced at his watch. "We haven't got all day, you know."

"I bring friendly greetings," commenced Vogel. "As a matter of fact, Sivuyile Gqabe ..."

"That snake," snorted Zeena. "We thought as much."

"No, really," replied Vogel hurriedly. "He's prepared to compromise, you see. I think you'll find that what Sivuyile has to suggest about the bones is, in fact, incredibly ..."

"Mac," Marc held up a hand. "You disappoint me. You've changed, man. No lies. It's shocking, actually. Otherwise, why should you act as go-between for that slimy careerist bastard?"

Zeena snapped, "I told you, Marc. These people never change. See, they gang up now, the whites and the blacks - just to squeeze us out."

"So much for old comrades, eh?" agreed her husband.

"Marc, Zeena, listen," said Vogel desperately. "Sivu's okay, he's ..."

"He's a fat capitalist pig," said Marc flatly.

Zeena sneered, "The radical black lawyer."

Marc nodded, "Rich, famous, his name in the newspapers, appears on television - jets around the world to conferences on human rights, and works for big American corporations. Why? Hah! Because, *boet*, he's black."

There was a tap at the window. The two men in identical grey suits stood outside, peering in. One gestured apologetically to his watch.

"*Ons kom*," yelled Zeena.

"Mac, we don't care what compromise that black swine is offering. We will dictate terms, not them." Marc Hendricks shrugged. "That's why I agreed to meet you, comrade. You can help in this new struggle, see. You must give me Sivuyile's security police file."

Vogel was stunned. He had not expected this abrupt turn in the discussion. Vogel didn't know what to reply. He stared out of the window. The archivist studied the cropped, matching haircuts of the men outside. They looked like off-duty policemen. The smaller one, he noticed, had a pistol stuck casually into his trouser waist at the front. A reckless thought struck him: could the Hendricks be mixed up with the recent bombings?

"We're in a hurry," declared Zeena. "When can you give us that file?"

Vogel hesitated. "How'd you know about these files anyway?"

She replied coolly, "Nothing happens in any government department in the Western Cape without us knowing about it."

Marc Hendricks laughed. "See, the *bruin mense* are everywhere."

"Well?" demanded Zeena. "Do we have a deal, Mr. Vogel?"

"There'll be things in Gqabe's police file that will, I have no doubt, be very useful to us," explained Marc. "It will be worth your while, comrade."

"Sorry," said Vogel. "But those documents really are confidential."

"White people," Zeena exhaled scornfully. "Still sitting on the fence."

"Actually," added Vogel, "there is no file on Sivuyile, anyway."

"Man, but you changed, Macaulay," remarked Marc Hendricks sadly. "Part of the establishment, eh? Or currying favour with your new bosses?"

"He's a courier," sneered Zeena. "Messenger boy for the black *baas*."

"Come," said Marc loudly and moved towards the door. In the hallway, Marc murmured softly, hurriedly, "Is there a file on me?"

Vogel was startled. Why did Marc Hendricks not want his wife to hear? He also seemed embarrassed. Vogel shook his head.

Outside the two bodyguards stepped back when the front door opened and glared at the archivist as he emerged. Zeena nodded to the bodyguards and sighed ostentatiously, "They're all the same, these white people."

The day had turned murky. Vogel struggled down the path as a rising wind flung dust in his eyes and corkscrewed plastic refuse through the air.

He drove home swiftly: Settlers Way, De Waal Drive, Jutland, Mill, Annandale, then right into Hatfield, where he parked. The difference was everywhere around him. It was there in the names of homes, offices, public buildings and streets. Officially, lawfully, racial definitions had been erased from the map. But such distinctions still manifestly defined most of the contours and divisions of the city, and were even etched on people's faces, drawing an invisible line between the powerful and the weak.

That night the tempest finally broke. Rain blew sideways. Vogel felt convulsive squalls shiver the walls of his home. He stayed indoors all Friday as the gale rampaged across the slim peninsula, uprooting telephone poles, battering fishing boats and yachts and pulverizing hundreds of tin shacks.

Vogel had said nothing when Zeena sighed, "They're all the same, these white people." He remained silent as he walked to the gate, though he heard her hiss something. Then louder, bolder, he heard Marc Hendricks too.

"Racist!"

Fourteen

SUNRISE unfurled, cleansed and sluiced. Smoky rays filtered over the mountaintop. By the time Vogel had driven round the bay and reached Bloubergstrand, the noonday light was so clear he could see the containers stacked on ships anchored far out, waiting to dock.

The view from the Xaba's flat was the classic picture postcard of Cape Town: an arc of snow-white sand in the foreground; then rising sheer across the choppy waters of Table Bay, the immensity of Table Mountain with the city curled under its prehistoric bulk.

Mary, as always, fussed over him protectively. Zechariah immediately re-ignited an irrational dispute that had rumbled on for nearly thirty years over their unfounded support for rival London football clubs. Neither had been abroad, let alone to the northern hemisphere or Britain, and Vogel had long forgotten why he'd given his unquestioned loyalty to Chelsea. He suspected it might be because Zech had chosen Arsenal and that this gave them something to scrap over. His own father Gershon, Vogel remembered, had supported Liverpool. But that was because, when a seaman, he had once docked there, and had actually watched the team play: an epic 3-2 victory that he described over and over, always concluding, "An' Liverpool didn't just conquer any team, boys, but Sir Matt Busby's Manchester United."

Zechariah's ferocious erudition for the minutiae of Arsenal's team selection and tactics made Vogel laugh. From the wall-length panoramic window of the Xaba's tiny one-bedroom flat he could see the brown hump of Robben Island in the middle of the bay, oddly convex and enigmatic in the lemony sunlight. The archivist wondered how Zechariah, after all he'd suffered there as a prisoner, could behave so freely, or laugh so unreservedly, whilst he, Macaulay Vogel - penalized

111

so absurdly little in contrast - still felt burdened with such anger. He was always amazed at the older man's gusto and humour. Vogel had once asked Zechariah how he could bear to live with such a view, however magnificent, of his own purgatory and incarceration.

"Because this," replied Zechariah simply, "was where Mary lived."

A white lawyer from Johannesburg, Mary had been assigned to defend Zechariah P. Xaba, and when he'd been condemned to Robben Island for thirteen years, she had simply bought a small flat in Bloubergstrand with a clear view of the island penitentiary and waited for his release, or the day of liberation, whichever came first. She was lean and angular, against Zech's hearty girth. Both were greying, handsome, and so seemingly at ease that Vogel, enviously, sometimes thought it was as if they shared the same ego.

Casually, after lunch, Zech asked, "You returned that file, eh?"

"Yeah," replied Vogel, accepting a brandy from Mary. "I did."

"Good," she said. "I don't want you keeping any more secrets from us."

Normally, and probably if it was anyone else, declared Zechariah, he would counsel that all the files be smuggled out of the castle and published immediately. The Xabas produced an inky, cheaply-printed slim pamphlet, *Umhlobo* (Friend), more like a samizdat. It appeared sporadically, whenever they had the funds, and was distributed at taxi-ranks or railway stations in outlying townships, Langa, Gugulethu, Khayelitsha.

"To teach our people to read between the lines," claimed Zechariah. However in this instance, he said, publishing the files was completely out of the question as the source would be too easy to identify.

"That's right," exclaimed Mary. "You could go to jail!"

"Macaulay?" asked Zechariah sternly.

Zechariah's father, the Rev. Japheth M. Z. Xaba, had been an Anglican priest serving several rural villages around Butterworth, and in moments of great seriousness Zech appeared to have inherited much of that measured, old world gravity. At such times Vogel - despite his habitual inclination for privacy, even concealment - felt an overwhelming urge to confess.

"I took the file back, I promise," vowed Vogel earnestly. "Then, just as I was about to slot it into the correct stack, I found the other one, the file I'd been searching for - you know, the dossier with all my personal details. It was right there, Zech, just like it was waiting for me, even though I'd turned the office upside down."

"Hang on. You mean, you now have *two* police dossiers?"

"Yeah."

"And you've removed both from the Castle?"

"Exactly."

"You can't do this, Mac," groaned Mary. "These are highly classified documents. Listen, I'm a lawyer. You are stealing government property."

"That's not the point," replied Vogel heatedly. "These are my secrets, Mary. This is about me, my life. These bloody documents are stuffed full of information about me - places, names, codes, dates, lots of things I don't even recognize or remember anymore whether they're true or not. This isn't just another professional archive job, see. It's about me, Macaulay Vogel. So actually, yes, I do think I've a right to look into this. I mean, you wouldn't believe all what's there, the things they snooped around, y'know ... personal things."

"Intimate?" asked Mary softly.

There was silence. Vogel's eyes filled with tears.

"Recordings?" prompted Zechariah. "Transcripts?"

Mary sat on the arm of his chair, her head against his, hair brushing against his face. "Marda?"

He nodded. He felt the suppleness of fresh-rinsed curls nuzzle his ear.

"It's alright, Mac," she murmured. "There's no shame in this, love."

"I see her everywhere." Vogel paused. "In the street, shops, cafés." It was hard for him to get the words out without unleashing tears. "Mary, I can see her, *exactly* as she was. I just can't get this out of my mind, you see."

The burnished afternoon, framed in the window, was stilled: the chaste, sapphire sky flawless, the mountain on the other side of the bay as familiar and unchanging as a photograph. Vogel gazed at the view, expressionless.

"You're having some sort of break-down, Mac," said Mary softly.

"It's been a long time coming. We could see it. Time to let Marda go, love."

He said fiercely, "You don't understand. This isn't about Marda, see. It's about me. What kind of a person I was ... that I am."

He turned to Zechariah, pleading, "Have I deluded myself all these years?"

"There's nothing to be ashamed of," said Zechariah. "You feel mucky, defiled. Believe me, I understand. But the ones who are really degraded are the people who did this, not you. Don't let them get back at you like this, man. You have to let go of the past."

"You knew me, Zech. Was I so ... self-centered? So utterly blind?"

"Don't do this, Mac. Quit flagellating yourself. They've still got a hold over you. Those swine put all sorts of garbage into their files. You know that. They were out of control, towards the end, those security cops, when their crude, petty world was disintegrating. They just stuck in all kinds of spiteful stuff, lies they knew would come back one day and crunch decent people."

"But some of it's true, eh?" insisted Vogel.

"Mac," whispered Mary, "we must move on."

The archivist looked defiantly from Zechariah to Mary. "But some of it is true," he repeated, eyes watery. "And if that's so, then what sort of a person does that make me?"

Zechariah said, "You were just an ordinary guy."

"They were extraordinary times," added Mary.

"That still doesn't excuse ..." Vogel's voice was harsh, choking. He began to cry. "I'm not who people think I am, you know."

"It was the times, Macaulay," muttered Zechariah embarrassed.

"You simply have to let go," instructed Mary, gripping Vogel's trembling shoulder. "Please, Macaulay. Otherwise you'll go mad."

"But that's exactly what I did - put it out of my mind, forgot!" Tears dribbled onto his lip, brackish to the tongue, but his voice was clearer now the distress was unblocked. "It's all there, though, in the file. In black and white. The time, the place ... the person. CCT10/36, MB33, whatever."

Through a tearful haze, he saw Zechariah and Mary exchange glances.

"You sure you want us to hear this?" asked Mary. "Some things are better left …"

"No, I've lied to myself about this, all these years. Now I need to say it, admit it." His voice dropped to a whisper, "I betrayed Marda, you see."

Abruptly words gushed out in a surge, released after twenty-five years of acidic accretion. "It's in the file. There's no denying it. They'd sussed me out, totally, with every detail to prove it. I can't fool myself, Mary. It's all - all - in the file. My grubby deceit. The time, place … the woman. The cops knew me better'n I know myself." Involuntarily Vogel snickered and sniffed simultaneously, almost choking. "I'd even forgotten her name, you see."

Vogel paused expectantly, waiting for the anger, their censure.

Eventually Zechariah asked, "Who was it?"

Vogel blushed. "Well, the report claims that she wasn't even a natural blonde." He added bitterly, "And her reference number was CW6/12."

"Macaulay," interrupted Mary quickly. "You need professional help with this."

"Mary, how could I have simply wiped that out of my mind? Okay, it was right at the beginning, and it only happened once. All the same, this did happen - and I forgot about it, completely. Rubbed that memory right out."

"That was twenty-five years ago, for God's sake. Marda would …"

"And if I erased something like that, what else am I hiding?"

"Look, love, you have to forgive yourself too, you know."

The archivist felt a vinegary, sickly taste scour his already constricted throat. "Mary, I'm not who you think I am."

She took his hand and pressed it to her cheek. Vogel saw that her eyes were brimming.

"Aren't you ashamed of me?" he asked.

She shook her head. He turned to Zechariah desperately. "Zech?"

"Marda loved you. That's all you need to know."

Decisively Mary interjected, "What Macaulay needs now, Zechariah, is protection. He needs the help of influential friends."

Vogel had been slow to react as Mary and Zechariah seemed to talk about him as if he wasn't present. Then he heard Zechariah saying, "You're right, it's perfect. I'll ring tomorrow and fix a meeting with Leonard Barr."

"Lenny and Mac go back a long way," enthused Mary. "Then there's also the connection with Grethe. That'll help."

"Grethe?" asked Vogel, puzzled.

"Grethe Cilliers," explained Mary patiently, as if he were simple. "Grethe has lots of influence. For sure, Grethe will want to help as well."

Vogel was baffled. "But what's Grethe got to do with Lenny?"

"Oh Macaulay, you're such a hermit,' Mary chided. She spoke carefully, guarded, more now as though enlightening an impressionable child. "Lenny and Grethe have lived together for years, they're an item."

"What happened to Rhoda?"

"It was only a stepping stone marriage for him, I guess. No primary school teacher could compete with a TV star. Not as radical as Geoff Tycott, mind you, who shucked his nice white Rosebank wife for an up-and-coming black businesswoman. Still, Lenny's moving up in the world. He's a player."

"They're partners in business, too," added Zechariah.

"In business?"

"Lenny's on the board of Grethe's TV production company."

When they spoke there seemed, to Vogel, to be a delay before the words reached him, like a conversation on a faulty long-distance line.

Zechariah said, "I'll ring Lenny tomorrow, arrange a meeting."

"No, please," exclaimed Vogel. This came out shrill, more alarmed than he'd intended. "Thank you," he added hastily. "But I don't think so."

"Lenny's an M.P., Mac, a big cheese these days," said Zechariah. "He'll know what to do."

"Thing is," admitted Vogel, "I went to see Grethe the other day ..."

Zechariah placed his arm round the archivist's shoulder and squeezed hard. "Leave it to me, Mac. Lenny's really the answer, believe me."

116

Mary smiled, "Time to step out of the dark, love, and let in the light."

Three hours later, glowing with brandy, slightly unsteady on his feet, but no longer tearful, Vogel hugged Zechariah and Mary effusively. They had not yet turned on any lights and the room was growing dark. The setting sun flickered threads of silver sparkles across the seal-grey sea.

"You boys drink too much," chided Mary mildly. She hadn't drunk a drop herself in nearly eighteen years, ever since Zechariah's release from prison. She was a recovering alcoholic.

The archivist hovered in the doorway, his thoughts sluggish and brandy-dulled. Behind Mary, he noticed, the mountain had been swallowed into the dusk and the lights of Cape Town flickered prettily across the bay.

It was only the next morning as he strode up Signal Hill, Sunday-silent and breathing in the caustic sea air, that he remembered the parting remark from Mary in the darkened doorway. He had become aware of a gentle but insistent tug at his arm. "Zech's drinking heavily again," Mary whispered hurriedly. "Please don't encourage him, Mac."

As the archivist made his way unsteadily along the outside corridor towards the ill-lit communal stairwell, Zechariah had joined Mary in the open doorway and shouted out, jarringly loud in the night's quiet, "Beware Minister Biyela, Mac. I know him well. He is a man who loves secrets."

It had been strange to hear that solemn preacher-like voice struggling to articulate carefully. "Zechariah means 'Yahweh remembers' and I never forget, you see. *Bhuti*, beware the Deputy Minister. That D.K. Biyela is too ambitious. Yho! Who knows? A white scapegoat ..."

It was a blue, crunchy autumn day. A lisp of breeze ruffled the sluggish bay. As the archivist's brandy-fugged mind eased, he brooded over Zechariah's earlier caution, "You need to be careful, Mac, even talking to old friends about those files. People will suspect your motives."

Then as he had lurched down the stairs, Zechariah had yelled, "Hey!"

Vogel had stopped, leaning against the wall.

Zech's cheerful voice echoed through the concrete stairwell. "Was there anything about me in your files?"

"No," Vogel called back. "No, absolutely nothing."

Vogel reached the crest of Signal Hill. In the docks, an imperious, icing white Nordic cruise ship glistened, tiered like a wedding cake.

Everywhere he turned, Vogel reflected, he was being trapped by his own deceit - even when he was attempting to be candid, or simply kind. It wasn't precisely a lie that he'd told Zechariah. He had not come across any dossier, after all, exclusively on Zechariah Xaba. Yet it was also not strictly true either. In dozens of other files Vogel had come across references to him.

Many of these annotations, in fact, were entirely contradictory.

Put together, however, the scraps of information about Zechariah formed an unflattering portrait. There were slivers of fact, shards of truth, but no likeness emerged of the man himself. The scale and generosity of Zechariah P. Xaba was entirely absent. Instead there was an unrecognisable kaleidoscope of fragments scattered at random: BLGK, NQT and W and Y and Z. But no X for Xaba. The personality was missing. There was plenty of tittle-tattle and nudging innuendo about alleged amorous adventures as well as numerous mentions of his unhappy first wife Nomtombeko. There was even a chilly titillation when reports lapsed into algebraic shorthand, "EL451 has abandoned KWT7/23 and currently co-habits with UM8/269."

Was he going to tell Zechariah that, in front of Mary? There had also not been a single reference to his big laugh, his constancy and courage or his resolute loyalty and kindness; no mention that Zech had been tortured, many times over, yet still preserved such munificence of spirit and sweetness.

All the same, Vogel had dissembled with his friend.

Fifteen

HE agreed with Zechariah: secrecy corroded everything and so, Vogel supposed, those files in the Castle, and all the other secret documents, should be published, purged by being exposed to the light. Yet in the end those to benefit most from this might be the very agents who had in fact compiled the offending dossiers, while the people who risked most hurt and distress from such openness could be the victims of all that snooping. What harm would really come to a general or secret policemen of the *ancien regime* if the full measure of their brutality and mendacity were disclosed? Revelations about known bastards, reflected the archivist, would come as no surprise; in some instances, it might even enhance their already gruesome reputations.

He thought of Colonel Boschard, once head of their local secret police, who now ran his own 'security consultancy.' If the full measure of Boschard's skilled ruthlessness became public knowledge, it would probably only add to his commercial cachet. On the other hand, if a reasonably decent person were to have malevolent tittle-tattle repeated, the result could be devastating. If Boschard were exposed as a villain, so what? He'd profit. But if even some of the trivial details which Vogel read daily about Boschard's victims were to be uncovered, they'd be tainted forever, diminished in everyone's eyes - maybe their own, too - whether that anecdote in the dossier was accurate or had been maliciously planted. What, for example, would be the upshot if unverified gossip about Zechariah Xaba were to be made public?

Files, cursed the archivist, did indeed have a life of their own.

He had no idea what to do. Vogel felt he was being lured far, far out of his depth. When the telephone rang on Sunday afternoon he was relieved to hear the urbane, confident voice of Leonard Barr.

Lenny had been his direct superior in their clandestine network, and even in the worst crisis Lenny had always remained cool. Lenny was a strategic thinker. Lenny would know what to do; yes, Lenny would certainly have sound advice.

"Everyone's talking about you, Macaulay," chided Leonard Barr. His voice was crisp. He could also sound abrasive in his brevity. "Got yourself into bit of a mess, eh?" Vogel wondered if he was referring to his visit to Grethe Cilliers. Then Lenny added, "Both Sivuyile and Zechariah called. They want me to see you. I can give you an hour, at twelve thirty tomorrow. Are you still living in that shitty little house in Gardens? Then it will take less than five minutes to walk to Parliament. You can have lunch with me, in the M.P.'s dining room. So do me a favour, hm, and wear a jacket and tie."

At the appointed hour, however, as Vogel crossed the grey cobbled courtyard in front of the lofty, columned building, he detected Leonard Barr standing on the top step of the entrance to Parliament, scanning approaching visitors anxiously. He wore a russet tweed jacket and forceful yellow cravat. Even when a trade union organizer, Lenny had stood out with his sartorial flair and that expensively educated, almost exaggeratedly British accent. His finely sculpted face was, Vogel noticed, almost ashen, as if Leonard seldom ventured out into the sun, and his curled red hair was peppered with grey.

Leonard spotted the archivist and loped athletically down the steps.

"We have half an hour," he announced. "There's an urgent Security Committee meeting." He grasped Vogel by the elbow. "We'll go the Tea Garden instead. It'll be just like old times and our secret meetings."

They walked round the parliament building, past the stout, fenced-off statue of Queen Victoria, almost obscured by untended undergrowth, and turned into the Company Gardens. Lunchtime visitors idled through this public park in the brittle autumn sunshine. The statue of Cecil Rhodes remained boarded up, although above the temporary wooden screens, his raised left hand still pointed defiantly north. Lenny selected a table in the shade of a towering gum tree. In the past they'd often met here to exchange information, choosing a public place where they could not be overheard.

Lenny began decisively. "One's hearing strange things, Macaulay."

Vogel looked into his neutral malachite eyes. Was Lenny talking about Grethe Cilliers? He couldn't tell. He looked away, at a young couple playing chess. He thought of Marda.

"Reminds you of difficult days, eh?"

Vogel braced himself. He sighed. "Look, Lenny ..."

"Mac, Lenny was a trade unionist. I prefer Leonard now, thank you."

"Of course," said Vogel. He paused. "The thing is, Leonard ..."

"Stick to being an archivist," interrupted Leonard Barr. To a passing waitress, he hollered, "Two coffees. No milk, no sugar. We're in a hurry."

"Leonard ..."

"These are sensitive times, Macaulay."

"I went to see Grethe the other day and ..."

"As Marx said, history is not of man's choosing - well, words to that effect anyway." Leonard laughed and Vogel noticed his uneven teeth were heavily tobacco stained. "That's why I choose to sit on the backbenches, toil away on parliamentary committees. At this time in our history, us white folk shouldn't push ourselves forward too much, be too conspicuous. Otherwise you simply place yourself, so to speak, in the firing-line. Be content to be a kingmaker. Not the king, nor even a prince. Work in the background, Mac, that's my advice. There's a dialectic at work here, you see."

"Leonard," objected Vogel, "I'm not really interested in the dialectic right now."

"'*You may not be interested in the dialectic*,'" quoted Leonard. "'*But the dialectic is definitely interested in you.*'"

"Sorry?"

"Trotsky." Leonard Barr glanced at his watch. "I'm giving you frank, serious advice, Macaulay. Out there," he waved his hand northward, in the direction of the townships, "the situation's unstable. There's no work, not enough houses, a long drought. This is not the time to create waves. This morning there was another bomb ..."

"I didn't hear about that."

"You won't. It was defused in time. The Louis Botha statue, right in front of Parliament. See what I'm saying, Mac? As a pale male, this is the time to lie low. Stick to cataloguing the damn archive."

"Sivuyile told you about the files?"

"And Zechariah." He paused. "And, of course … Grethe." Leonard glanced at his watch again. "Where's that bloody coffee?"

"The thing is Lenny. Sorry, Leonard. The fact is I'd like to tell you, confess really, about something in the files. Should've done this ages ago." Leonard held up his hand. "Stop right there, pal. Spare me, please."

Vogel fell silent and for the first time wondered why the dapper Hon. Member of Parliament had not wanted, at the last minute, to take him to the M.P.'s dining room. Did Leonard Barr not wish to be seen with him now?

"For your sake, Macaulay, almost as much as for mine, I really don't want to know what you've found. Frankly, I don't think you understand the stakes. Because we've kept a lid on these things, not opened up the records, you can smear an opponent by merely insinuating they might've been a spy once - especially if people think you have access to inside info. This is the era of rumour and insinuation. Don't repeat this, but wanna know my pet name for Parliament? Paranoia Palace! As long as we don't know what's in the damn files, they remain lethal. Gossip, a sly hint - and careers are ruined, reputations soiled. Yup, access to secrets bestows power. Opportunities for blackmail. To shaft a rival. You getting the picture? Holy shit, Mac, haven't you ever wondered what D.K. Biyela's motives might be in all of this?"

"Well, no. Not really. I'm an archivist and …"

"And you report only to the Deputy Minister himself?"

"Yeah. Directly to Biyela, personally."

"And you are sworn to secrecy?"

"Of course. It's a highly sensitive issue. You can't just …"

"Mac, D.K.'s busy scrambling up the greasy pole. Maybe he's trying to find out if there's any dirt in those files that he can use, at the right time. And even if you don't find anything, the very fact that people are beginning to know about these classified records, and that D.K. might have access to secrets, potentially offers him huge influence and clout. Then there are the rumours about D.K. himself. They won't go away. You've heard them."

"No, I'm stuck in the archives. I don't hear much these days."

"That he was a spy himself."

"No, never … Biyela?"

"Who knows! It's just another rumour. But the very fact that D.K. has access to locked-up files gives him enormous power. The power of secrets."

"Hmm, I see. Gosh, no, I never thought about it that way. Amazing."

"I fear you will be swept away by currents that you don't understand."

"So what should I do?"

"Drop the whole thing. Hand the files back to D.K. Sign off and return to your normal job. Tell Biyela you haven't found anything interesting but insist it's too depressing to continue. Get a medical certificate or something. Tell him the dust in the files gives you asthma. But just bloody forget them."

"That's your advice? Simply … shelve the files? Forget everything!"

"Yeah, that's my sincere advice, Macaulay. I have to go."

"But Lenny, Leonard, wouldn't publishing the files …"

"Out of the question, way too risky."

"So … when?"

"When the time is right."

"And now? I must just keep quiet?"

"It's too soon, old man. Bad timing, you see."

The waitress arrived with two coffees. Leonard Barr waved her away and rose to go. "Trust me, comrade. Stick to being an archivist."

"Lenny," Vogel called out after him. "And Grethe's TV production company? You're saying … the time is right for cooking programmes?"

Leonard stopped, shrugged. "Frankly, I'm also following advice," he replied. "And you should take note of this, too. It's incredibly wise counsel, Mac. Absolutely the best plan, in fact." He grinned. "From Lenin himself."

Leonard Barr's strident voice resonated through the silky autumn air: "*When you live among the wolves you must howl like a wolf.*"

Sixteen

LIEUTENANT Nxumalo was outside his office door at the Castle the next morning. It was raining lightly. As the archivist reached the top of the stone stairway and stepped onto the rampart, Nxumalo turned and waved.

"Haven't seen you for days," called Nxumalo cheerily. "One was concerned." His green uniform was damp. He must have been out in this drizzle for a while. "I was coming to pay my respects. Check that our esteemed Dr. Vogel was okay."

Vogel stared at the soldier coldly, then took out his key chain. Had Nxumalo been listening at the door - or been attempting to open it, even force an entry? Normally the archivist had no trouble in unlocking his office straight away, but in his agitation he couldn't find the right key among the score or so that he kept on his congested chain. He fumbled with several unsuccessfully. Did Nxumalo, he wondered, have another key?

The archivist was aware of the soldier still talking as he pushed past him into the room. Vogel heard the lieutenant say, "We must have a coffee sometime," as he struggled to fit the key back into the lock and secure the door from the inside. "Or a beer," called Nxumalo. Vogel remembered an instruction from when he'd first joined his underground network: if arrested, don't chatter. Nervous babble is a sure give-away of nerves, if not guilt. He could hear Nxumalo still talking from the other side of the door. Eventually Nxumalo called out cheerfully, "*Ciao*," and Vogel listened to his footsteps recede on the stone parapet. The archivist sat down. He was shaking.

Vogel had run nearly all the way to the Castle. Because of the rain he'd taken the short cut. Given the early hour and dim light he'd thought he could sneak down Plein, past the diminished band of demonstrators, without being noticed. There had been less than twenty protesters, huddled round a brazier by the slave plaque, chanting disconsolately, "Leave the bones ..." at the few pedestrians who scurried by. Vogel was nearly at the corner when he heard the shout, "scum", followed by angry yells of "traitor" and "scab." He looked back. The subdued assembly, mostly hooded with anoraks, had turned to stare at him. Some shook their fists. Then he heard another cry, filled with revulsion. Several protesters began to move in his direction and Vogel broke into a run. Behind, he heard the hate-filled cry again: "Racist!"

The room was cold. He could smell a familiar reek of damp and mould; that dank, premature whiff of heaps of paper condemned to decay. He sat for a long time, listening to the rain on the flat roof. Slowly a clammy anxiety trickled, drip by remorseless drip, into his thoughts. At the time he had hardly paid attention because it seemed such a casual remark. But the more Vogel brooded over this, the more it seemed odd the way Leonard Barr had bounded down the steps of Parliament to cut him off. It was almost as if Lenny had been embarrassed to be associated with him.

Vogel tried to work, examine files, but Lenny's words kept slithering back, insinuating and unsettling. "Don't stir things up, Macaulay. Some people think you're trying to uncover an informer." He hadn't paid much attention at the time as it had seemed like an impromptu aside, and he'd put it down to playfulness or a perverse hint of spite when Lenny added, "But logically, if there was a leak, it would, most likely, be either you or Marda." And when Leonard Barr leaned across the table confidentially the archivist had imagined he was teasing. "And Mac, I hear rumours," he'd murmured, "that it was you ..."

Vogel remembered the tangy eucalyptus fragrance from the giant gum tree next to their café table. He'd imagined that Leonard Barr was being ironic, possibly sarcastic. The archivist stared in despair at the stacked files all around him, emanating their feeble smell of mouldering desolation.

He felt hemmed in, trapped. Normally when he studied documents there was a trail, however faint, where one detail eventually led to another, towards some sort of resolution, however tenuous. Here there was only unpredictability. The files seemed heavy and sullen. It was almost as if they were conspiring against him. The rain pounded harder on the roof and as he stared at the inert files he felt a frustrated sense of silent rage. Somewhere among those hundreds of documents was the decisive clue for which he was searching - yet the dossiers were maliciously withholding that information.

Vogel felt the accumulated presence of the files around him: animate, quiet ... waiting. Rain thrummed on the roof in rhythmic waves, as though drumming out sly messages. Listening to this fluctuating beat, the archivist wondered if files had a silent way of communicating. He had heard about the great mopane savannahs up north, where if buck, buffalo or elephant begin to browse on the mopane trees, their leaves react immediately by producing tannin and become far too bitter to eat - and then all the mopane trees within a close radius down wind promptly pick up this scented warning and also start to manufacture toxins, thus insulating themselves from attack.

He sat for hours staring at the files. Vogel tried not to think about it. All the same, Leonard Barr's seemingly offhand remark echoed, breathy and insistent, in his head: "But logically, if there was a leak, it would, most likely, be either you or Marda."

Like a tongue flickering over a decaying tooth unable to resist the lure of probing into putrefying cavities, however unpleasant, Vogel could not stop his thoughts coming back to one name. This name, whispered, slunk back, unbidden, again and again. He had not been an informer. So he could not silence that repetitive sigh; a sly, sinuous exhalation: Marda, Marda ...

MB33. What did that alphabetical riddle signify? Before transferring to Cape Town, Marda's family had lived briefly in Mossel Bay. Yet if RS identified a policy spy, or MI a link to Military Intelligence, then wasn't it also possible that MB could be a cryptogram for, say, Military Branch?

Space in the room seemed to shrink and files distend, as though engorged by damp and rain. Vogel felt overwhelmed by the mass of documents. He was encircled, unable to escape, steadily suffocating. He sensed he might be crushed at any moment by the menacing weight of indifferent records. The name hammered in his head like unrelenting rain.

Vogel forced himself to repeat, out loud, Paul's *Epistle to the Romans*: "Therefore thou art inexcusable, O Man, whosoever thou art that judgest ..."

On his way home the archivist bought a munificent bouquet of scarlet roses. The rain had dwindled to an unvarying sprinkle and a pale sun floated over Signal Hill. When Vogel reached Sabata Dalindyebo Way he looked up and saw a violently tinted rainbow arching back over the entire bay. Inside, he placed the flowers on the sideboard next to Marda's photograph.

This act of propitiation achieved nothing. The name pulsed in his head, merciless. The more he tried to force his mind blank the more it overflowed with just one thought, one word ... one name. Marda, Marda, Marda. It fell like lashing rain, splattering and indiscriminate, disordered and confused. Outside the steady downpour persisted all night, dislodging several slates from his roof and sluicing deep rivulets through Sabata Dalindyebo Way.

"Therefore thou art inexcusable, O man," he repeated over and over and over. "For wherein thou judgest another, thou condemnest thyself ..."

Seventeen

BOSCHARD SECURITY, with a view of cranes and gantries along the docks, was in the middle of a business-park just beyond the clutter of the main railway shunting yard. Vogel phoned for two days, at two hourly intervals, and a velvety-voiced receptionist assured him repeatedly that Mr. Boschard did indeed know exactly who he was and definitely, one hundred per cent, would call him back just as soon as he had finished his meeting.

The receptionist soon recognized Vogel's voice and would respond cheerily, "Tuliswa here," as if he had not already phoned a dozen times. "And how're we doing today, Dr. Vogel?"

The archivist became more disconcerted when he got through to Boschard's secretary. She sounded delighted to hear from him. After several calls they were on first name terms and Farida solicitously asked after his wellbeing as if they were old acquaintances.

"Mr. Boschard looks forward to speaking to you, Macaulay," she repeated unflappably. "Give him half an hour or so."

On the third day, Friday, when his first two calls of the morning had not been returned by eleven o'clock, Vogel resolved to drive unannounced to Boschard's agency. He was worn away by doubt, unnerved by the growing uncertainty. Suspicion burrowed into his mind. He was unable to block it. The name crept upon him, again and again: a crafty, sibilant hiss, and he could neither quell this insinuation nor forgive himself for allowing it.

Boschard, Vogel was convinced, was the only one who could reassure him and terminate the unbearable ambiguity.

By the time he reached the business-park, however, Vogel was flustered and tense. A journey that would normally take twenty minutes had required over two hours. As the archivist drove down Loop Street, aiming to pick up the overhead N1 freeway at the foreshore, he found his progress was obstructed by a massed procession crossing Wale Street. Backed-up traffic hooted petulantly. Police stopped the silent marchers every five minutes to let through another two or three cars. It took Vogel half an hour to approach the front of the procession where he could finally read placards for the huge rally that had halted outside the Provincial Legislature. Thousands crammed the road, filtering in from adjoining streets and tailing, he now saw, far up into the Bo-Kaap. As Vogel eased his car through the hushed crowd he experienced a moment of panic as two mute protesters waved their placards, 'Respect our bones' and 'The slaves arise', right in front of his windscreen.

The scale of the gathering and its unnatural silence upset Vogel. He felt he was trapped in a sealed bubble. Hushed marchers snaked up Loop, against the traffic. Many glared wordlessly at him, and as soon as he could, Vogel veered off into a side-street. A platoon of police, with helmets, batons, and Perspex shields, were lined along the narrow pavement. In unison and without apparent instruction the entire squad abruptly charged in front of his car. They sprinted down Bree Street. Vogel picked up speed and turned into Buitengracht. At once, however, streams of hooded young men poured out of adjacent side-streets. Some ducked behind parked cars to throw stones and bottles. A group of youths sprinted by, banging on Vogel's windscreen. Several policemen raised rifles to fire rubber bullets. He heard a splintered crash of glass. His heart thumped with familiar dread.

At the intersection of Strand, he smelt a caustic irritation of tear gas. It was another hour before Vogel reached his destination. He shook with the recollected terror of riots.

This was a sensation he had not experienced for many years, though once it had been an almost daily ugliness: a sticky combination of elation and dread, plus the acid stink of ammonia, exhilaration and sweated fear. Vogel's agitation was exacerbated by circling the monotonous streets of the business-park for another half an hour, lost among anonymous auto repair shops, spare part depots and identical stockrooms; a scrubby no man's land of warehouses and industrial units where most street names had been stolen or worn away. The archivist finally located Boschard Security in a grubby two-storey building that looked like one more panel-beating or spray-paint plant, and as he pulled open the grilled security gate he felt a chilled panic that he had not endured since being summoned to Caledon Square, twenty or more years before, the only time he had been hauled in for questioning.

Here, in contrast, was a brilliantly illuminated foyer with a stainless corporate sheen. A young receptionist with styled hair extensions looked up.

"Dr. Vogel!"

"You were expecting me?" Vogel was astonished.

"Our security cameras in the car park."

"But how did you know it was ..."

"Your license plate, Dr. Vogel. I ran a check." Tuliswa pointed to her computer screen and giggled. "One can't be too careful these days, hey?"

An older woman came down the stairs, heels clacking in the marbled tranquility. Her clothing was more homely. She wore a fluffed plaid woollen sweater and a fawn silk scarf on her head. "Macaulay," she called out warmly, extending a welcoming hand.

"Farida?"

"Mr. Boschard is aware you are here and ... aha!" A green light blinked on the receptionist's console. "Mr. Boschard will see you now."

He followed Farida up the curved marble steps. There was a surgically white-paneled corridor with several evenly-spaced sepia photographs of now almost certainly vanished Cape Dutch farmsteads. Farida stopped at the first door and immediately Vogel pulsed with an old terror, similar to the fright he had suffered in the streets when faced with unknown, visored authority.

The archivist recognized Boschard right away. He'd never met him, but several years before he'd seen Boschard's photograph in the social pages of a local magazine. The former security policeman had posed awkwardly between a glamorous female sports celebrity and a prominent Johannesburg casino magnate. Vogel had been astonished to read in the caption that this had been a party to mark the launch of Boschard Security.

Boschard was much shorter and plumper than Vogel had imagined. He had a pale, slightly anxious oval face and thinning gingery hair and wore a sleeveless tartan pullover. He inhaled on an unlit pipe. Next to him stood a muscular, shaven-headed African man in a bespoke three-piece worsted suit.

Boschard took the unlit pipe out of his mouth and waved at his paper-cluttered desk. "You will despair of me, Dr. Vogel." He spoke softly, with close cropped vowels. "As an archivist, I am sure that you prize clarity and tidiness above all else." Boschard's office was chaotic. There were open telephone directories and, spread across the floor, large-scale maps of the city, while print-outs, newspaper clippings, scraps of paper and ring-bound ledgers were strewn over his desk and on top of the steel filing cabinets against the wall.

Boschard regarded Vogel shyly, with an avuncular and reflective interest. "One hears a great deal about the paper-free office, but ..."

"This is not what I expected," muttered Vogel uncomfortably.

"Yes," agreed Boschard. He also seemed puzzled. Quickly, as if recollecting his manners, he turned to the man beside him and announced with a wave of his pipe, "This is my associate, Mr. Mxolisi Mkapta."

"Welcome, sir," greeted Mr. Mkapta, pumping Vogel's hand warmly. Turning back to Boschard, he added, "S'okay chief, I'm on the case."

Boschard chuckled as soon as Mxolisi Mkapta had exited. "You will notice that us sleuths love to talk just like the TV police shows, I'm afraid."

The archivist couldn't think of anything to say. Time seemed to hover.

On the untidy desk he noticed a picture of two freckled, ginger-haired teenage girls, possibly twins. They were in ungainly school uniforms, posing in a garden with a mottled elderly spaniel. All at once, Vogel felt exhausted.

Farida clucked sympathetically. "I'll leave you two to catch up, hey?" Closing the door, she called, "Don't forget, you have a two-fifteen, Mr. B."

Boschard hesitated, apparently unsure how to proceed. He stuck the pipe back in his mouth and sucked pensively.

"This is not what I expected," repeated Vogel awkwardly.

"Farida looked after you okay then?'

"Thank you."

"Tuliswa too?"

"Very charming."

"Good, good." Boschard rapped his pipe against the silver ash-tray, although there was nothing in the pipe to clear out.

Vogel could not shake the strange sensation of drowsiness that seeped through his limbs. Perhaps this is a delayed shock from trying to dodge the rioters and tear gas, he thought. He wondered if his face was flushed.

Boschard was the name they had always been able to put to the faceless terror of the state. For as long as Vogel could remember this man had commanded the specialized police branch which monitored local dissident activity. It was Colonel Boschard, or so the legend claimed, who had been responsible for Edwin Sarkissian's arrest and Zechariah Xaba's capture and long imprisonment. Boschard had also supervised the torture of Rafik's partner 'Billy' - and, after Billy broke, had orchestrated the consequent butchery of Billy's entire underground cell. Rumour and shocking tales greedily fastened themselves to Boschard, spreading his infamy among underground networks, attributing to the Colonel a terrifying combination of prodigious cunning and pitiless cruelty. The longer the policeman had remained faceless, the more bloodcurdling had become this image.

The archivist became aware Boschard was gesticulating with his pipe.

"Dr. Vogel, will you not sit, please?"

"This is not what I expected," repeated Vogel, sitting.

Boschard chuckled. "Me, too."

"Sorry?"

"All the same, pleasing don't you find - after all this time?"

"Actually, this is extremely odd for me. I'm still rather ... upset. It was difficult getting here, you see. The fighting in town, the tear gas ..."

Boschard plumped into the swivel chair on the other side of the desk and declared, "Mountain spring water." He rotated his chair and selected a terracotta pitcher and crystal glass from the trolley behind him. "Bottled on my farm, guaranteed pure. Swallowed in one, they say, this will help settle the nerves." He watched approvingly as Vogel drank the water in one single gulp. "That's it. Bushmen worshipped its healing qualities, I believe."

The phone rang. Boschard had to clear away a newspaper to reach the receiver. "No calls please, Tuli - I'm in a meeting till my two-fifteen."

Boschard grimaced contritely. "In the corporate environment, one becomes a slave to clock watching, Dr. Vogel." He glanced at the clock on the wall. "But one's clients pay through the nose for such billable time."

"You want me to pay for this?" exclaimed Vogel in alarm.

"Heavens, Dr. Vogel, I'm joking! You are my guest. Alas, I fear you fellows - you, Edwin, Rafik and the others - imagined we modest security policemen were sadistic, literal-minded thugs with no sense of humour. Am I right? Just a little bit, eh?" Vogel noticed lines of deep bluish discoloration under Boschard's eyes, the wages of insomnia.

Vogel coughed nervously. "This is very painful for me, Colonel ..."

"It's Dr. Boschard, by the way, though one doesn't like to advertise the fact too much." Boschard shrugged ruefully. "Sometimes, in my business, it is more constructive for people to imagine that one is a bit of a ruffian." Boschard leaned forward. "I confess, even so, that one would have preferred, given the choice, to follow a scholarly vocation." He gazed at the archivist, preoccupied. "In fact, I suspect we share much in common, you and I."

Vogel sensed his cheeks reddening. "Dr. Boschard, let me assure you that I do not normally simply barge in, unannounced. Nevertheless ..."

"I'm truly sorry about your loss," declared Boschard gently. "My condolences, sincerely. Please, you cannot know how much I personally empathize." At close range his unblinking eyes - olive irises flecked with yellow tints - appeared melancholy, perhaps from exhaustion. "It's important for me to tell you this, Dr. Vogel. I do understand your suffering, you see."

"What?" Vogel was startled. "What've you heard?"

"That this should happen, finally, after so long. We were all worried at the time, believe me. But it's too much that you should relive that loss afresh." Boschard pointed to the photograph on his desk of the teenage girls. Now that Vogel looked closer he could see the snap was slightly faded, the sun-lit colours visibly blanched with age. "I understand grief. I always felt I understood you, identified with your pain. Yes, and at the time, I should very much have liked to extend my sympathies, but in the circumstances ..."

He rose and awkwardly put a hand on Vogel's shoulder. "Doctor, permit me now to extend my deepest sorrow regarding your wife."

Vogel started. "But Marda wasn't my ..."

"Ah, but that's the way one always thinks of her, no? Yes, such a tragic, senseless loss. We policemen, despite what you think, understood your anguish. So naturally I am desolate to hear of your recent breakdown."

"My? What have you ... where have you been hearing such rubbish?"

"Dr. Vogel, I am a security consultant. The market leader, as we like to say nowadays. I keep my ears to the wind, you see. Or is it finger to the wind? I'm never quite sure of the correct English idiom."

"Ear to the ground," corrected Vogel.

"Precisely. And what one hears, on the ground, is that there is much, ah, consternation - is that the right word? - regarding your crusade. If truth be told, upsetting old comrades and ... others. Goodness, Dr. Vogel, finally you have succeeded in uniting people who were once bitter enemies! Oh yes, they are all horribly anxious about what might turn up in those old files."

"Look, I'm not allowed to talk about them," responded the archivist irritably. "They're classified. The real reason for my visit, in fact ..."

"Ah, files - our true love, eh? That, I hope one can state without fear of contradiction, is what yokes us together. Our reverence, if I may term it so, for documents, reports and archives. Am I not correct, Dr. Vogel? Different perspectives, perhaps - but absolute respect for the assembling of detail, fact, observation. No, the *scrupulous* assembling of such information. Otherwise there is only muddle and blunder." Boschard stuck the pipe back in his mouth and sucked on it hungrily. Air vacuumed through the empty bowl. "As a policeman one was - is

- all too aware, alas, of the foibles of one's informants. The human fallibility of our records, Dr. Vogel! Which is why I envy you. All the time you need, as a scholar, to prowl through the records, weeding out stupidity, sloppiness and deceit. For me, neglect of a dossier is a dreadful crime. It's destruction, a tragedy. For without reliable information, what do we have? Error, confusion - chaos!"

Boschard paused to rap his empty pipe against the silver ashtray again.

Brusquely Vogel demanded, "In the files, the letters CCT refer to central Cape Town, don't they?"

"That, if I remember correctly, was your designation. CCT10/36."

"Then why didn't you arrest me, Dr. Boschard? I've seen what you had on file. You could have put me away for years."

"We have much in common, Vogel. Maybe it was, I don't know ..."

"You thought I would lead you to others."

Boschard shrugged. "Perhaps I was protecting you."

"Or was the plan to blackmail me?"

"Did you ever consider that, hm ... simple human compassion?"

"And who was providing you with this information?"

Unruffled, Boschard replied, "I wouldn't assume, one should never assume, that there is only one source."

"And the code MB - what does that reveal?"

"Ah, of course! Now I see what troubles you."

"Was it ..." Vogel's voice faltered. "Was it ...?"

"Chaos, that's what we face, Dr. Vogel. A moth flaps its wings and half way round the world there's a landslide. Or is it a butterfly and an earthquake? I can never remember. Anyway, details, you see - one more detail doesn't always help, as you know. On the other hand, it might just be the one, however insignificant, that finally sets off an avalanche."

He pointed his unlit pipe at the archivist. "There were two more bombs this morning, Bonteheuwel and Muizenberg. Small ones, no one injured. Were these just random acts, hm, two isolated expressions of frustration? It could even be the work of one obsessive individual with a grievance - like you, say. Or is this something altogether more sinister, a deliberate plot to whip up discontent and provoke social mayhem?"

"You work for the government?"

"I serve the state, not governments." Boschard's voice was fastidious, almost reproachful. "Do not confuse a principal, Dr. Vogel, with mere politicians. You, more than anyone, should understand this. Order, for both of us, is sacrosanct. You classify, categorize, systematise. But at present you have a problem with your archives at the Castle, do you not? Some high officials of the past regime, to protect themselves, pilfered state files. They imagined such secrets might safeguard them from … a future trial, perhaps, for crimes committed against our new government? However in their panic and ignorance, these officials grabbed dossiers indiscriminately. As a result, your entire collection is unsystematic - hopelessly slapdash. A nightmare, anarchy. You see? We are, if you like, comrades in arms after all. In my modest way, I police the present while you, Dr. Vogel, patrol the past."

Vogel glanced at the clock on the wall. He was conscious his time was running out. "Dr. Boschard," he repeated fiercely, "who betrayed me?"

The melancholy olive-green eyes focused on the archivist. Boschard sucked on his empty pipe meditatively.

"Y'know," he chuckled, "you could always hire me to find out."

"D.K. Biyela," said Vogel angrily. "Deputy Minister Biyela. Did he hire you?"

"The problem is, bluntly - what did you expect to change? People? Human nature? Oh, that goes on regardless. But then you idealists feel let down! Instead, it is you that has changed. But you don't want to admit this. No, not at all! So now you cast about for someone - or something else - to blame."

"Everyone thinks I'm searching for a suspect. But, truthfully, I'm really only trying to find out about myself."

Boschard smiled timidly. "Do you know the work of Fernando Pessoa, the glorious Portuguese poet? A hobby of mine. Pessoa was brought up in Durban, you know. So this may interest you, Dr. Vogel - after Pessoa returned to Lisbon he wrote letters to all his friends and teachers back in Natal, pretending to be a psychiatrist, Dr. Faustino Autunes, and he asked each one of them for their impressions of …" Boschard clapped his hands together delightedly, "young Fernando Pessoa!"

Vogel hesitated. "Did he ever find out what he wanted to know?"

Boschard spread out his arms, and declaimed softly, tenderly: "*The traveller is the journey. What we see is not what we see but who we are.*"

"You read poetry?" asked Vogel incredulously.

"After a day studying repetitive, turgid reports, it cleanses the palate. Also, don't you find it instructive that the three great poets of the twentieth century all had terribly dull, backroom trades? T.S. Eliot worked in a bank in London, Constantine Cavafy toiled as a clerk for thirty years in the Irrigation Service of the Ministry of Public Works in Alexandria, while Pessoa ... poor, neglected, solitary Fernando Pessoa earned a pittance translating business letters for commercial concerns in Lisbon." Boschard beamed. "The point is, Dr. Vogel, that great dreams cannot survive without such tedious backroom labour ... which is why, of course, when our Special Branch operatives succeeded in infiltrating subversive organizations they usually rose rapidly within your underground ranks. Most of you lefties were chaotic, too busy staying up all night drinking and talking up grand visions of a utopian future or sleeping with each other's girlfriends. Our guys, on the other hand, were efficient and meticulous administrators - so soon got delegated exactly those humdrum tasks which meant that half the time we knew precisely what you were up to! Frankly, it's not so different today. Many of your old associates, now they're in power, still get carried away with fine speeches and forget, say, to deliver text books to schools."

"And where do you fit into all this, today?"

"A nuts and bolts man."

"But one," observed Vogel bitterly, "who sometimes still has to use his pliers to pull out the fingernails of anyone who gets in the way?"

Boschard sighed regretfully. "*What we see is not what we see but who we are.*" He pointed his pipe accusingly at Vogel. "You, I believe, also have the sensibility of a poet, Dr. Vogel."

"Me? Not at all. I'm much too prosaic. No, my temperament is far better suited to the humdrum prose of the archives."

"Oh? But I was always under the impression that you were the author of *Black Petals*."

"You are working for Deputy Minister Biyela," shouted Vogel angrily. "Admit it, D.K. Biyela hired you to keep an eye on me. He must have!"

"Dr. Vogel, go cautiously. Don't concern yourself with things beyond your competence. This business of secret files, it's becoming horribly messy. The public thinks most files were either destroyed or are safely locked away. But I know my colleagues. We are secretive people, wary and distrustful by nature. We hoard, we store. So they all squirreled away records, hid them in their brother's loft or buried them in a suitcase at the bottom of the mother-in-law's garden. Information, secrets ... it's the new currency, Dr. Vogel. Most of my colleagues - ah yes, both former and present agents - consider stashing away secret information as, well, let's call it insurance. Back-up, a safety net. A pension, even. And then they circulate rumours - such as, this or that government minister used to be a police spy."

"You do work for D.K. Biyela," repeated Vogel fiercely.

"Shame, you've been buried among those moldering archives far too long! Really, one mustn't believe everything one hears. And you used to be such an optimist, a quality I once envied. But I see, regrettably, you have been infected with the inherent pessimism of my secretive profession. We always assume the worst of everyone. In your case, that would be a terrible error, a grave mistake. Like losing your soul. Save yourself, Dr. Vogel."

"Then, tell me, who spied on me? Who gave you the information for your files?"

"In my experience, Dr. Vogel, a person is most often let down by themselves. Oh, people cast around for scapegoats. A suspect always asks, 'who gave the game away?' But trust me - and I have some aptitude in these matters - one generally betrays oneself." Boschard placed the unlit pipe back in his mouth and drew heavily, contemplating the archivist affectionately. "You are spreading uncertainty, Dr. Vogel. People are jumpy, fearful. Some things should remain buried. Those *laftige* slave bones, for example. Look what happens when you dig up skeletons and try to make sense of them today? Discontent, disorder! The files, you see, are like those bones. Best left to rest. Only to be seen by scholars, like you. Yes, classify and evaluate by all means. Bring order to the past, of course. But, please, leave the present to me, eh? Stick to your archives, Dr. Vogel."

The telephone on his desk rang. "Ah, my two-fifteen." His weary green eyes blinked. "Farida will show you out."

He waved his pipe in farewell. "Remember, Dr. Vogel, discretion!"

Boschard shrugged, "Files can take on a life of their own, y'know."

Eighteen

RAIN drizzles into every fissure. Wet gobs ooze under draughty doors and dribble below flaking sills of bolted windows. Rain slants. It soaks, it seeps. Cape Town seems lost, cut off. Squalls huff and surge. Damp sponges the city. Saline mists slither over the fragile peninsula, carved into the winter pitching Atlantic as if about to snap off from the rest of Africa. Perhaps this is what the first colonists experienced when they settled so far from Europe, severed from the world they knew. Tiny grains of grit leach from Vogel's eyes. Tear ducts trickle but they do not weep. He feels that he is oozing too. Vitality and emotion filter out, stealthily drip away. They leak, they seep.

All weekend the archivist dithers. He wanders into his kitchen to make a snack, walks straight out again, disgusted at the thought of food. His moods are unstable. He is irritable; skin scratchy and clammy. He loses his temper with inanimate objects. One moment he is apprehensive, the next overcome with lethargy. Fatigue creeps over him, a pervasive listlessness.

On Saturday afternoon he lies down on the sofa, covered in a woollen blanket to keep warm, and wakes hours later in the inky dark, the empty house chilled and rain still pounding on the slate roof. He moves to his bed and sleeps for hours. On Sunday he wakes late but feels even more worn out than when he went to bed the previous night. His eyes are reddened and runny.

He cannot avoid the repetitive, chronic doubt. He thinks only of this. Suspicion colonises his mind. Distrust drips out, unbidden. It resurfaces at improbable moments. Indecision leaks and seeps all weekend.

When he eats, food dissolves to unbearable, tasteless mush. He senses toxins gradually spread throughout his bloodstream. He is tormented by his uncertainty: what does he really know of Marda? The venom percolates and takes possession, infiltrates his mind and fouls his body.

He cannot believe anything is fixed. Everything seems to ooze and dissolve. Even his eyes are clogged with grainy secretions. Vogel keeps returning to stare at the black and white photo of Marda. When he is away from this photograph he cannot imagine her features anymore. He can see the dark twirl of hair, but not the face. What colour were her eyes? It is a formless, faded blur. Nothing is fixed.

His family home, which shivers and groans under this downpour, has changed. His own street, Sabata Dalindyebo Way, has altered. The neighbourhood is transformed. He, too, has changed.

Everything rises to the surface, pounded by unrelenting rainfall. Unseen cascades spurt from the mountainside, slashing out trees and undergrowth. Grubby torrents swirl down Sabata Dalindyebo Way, flushing away secreted stockpiles of builders' rubble and family garbage. On beaches and bays the roiling sea heaves up its noxious wreckage, hurling out the corroded entrails of yachts and fishing fleets among dense tangles of kelp.

Nothing stays still. Gummy residues filter from his eyes. Toxins leak from his skin. Dank fears sift to the surface of his mind. He has no control.

On Monday it takes him an hour to get up. Although he has slept for nine hours he is sluggish and exhausted. His eyes are inflamed with dry discharge. He feels listless and grubby, as if he has woken with a hangover despite not having drunk alcohol for days. He sets out for the Castle in the obdurate downpour, hoping that the sedating balm of routine may finally expunge this unrelenting cycle of uncertainty. Rain sluices into every cavity.

Nothing can resist the dousing rain. In Spin Street a huge gathering swarms round the building site. They are kept at bay by a cordon of police. In the dawn-grey light those astonished few who had endured a nocturnal vigil observed that the pounding rain had washed away clay topsoil in the construction trench and scores of bones had been rinsed to the surface.

The crowd is tense. People on their way to work stop to join the throng. There is also what looks like an entire, yellowing skeleton.

"It's a miracle," someone whispers.

They chant with renewed vigour: "The bones live."

Distorted by loudspeaker, Vogel hears a familiar voice: "The bones have spoken."

Rain pounds the Castle. The level of the moat has risen. A sheen of grey-green greasy algae ripples on the surface. Puddles flood the ramparts. Water slides under the ill-fitting door of his office and insinuates along the square window panes. Moisture stains the walls. A faint odor leaks from the files: a coagulating scent of mildew and decomposition. Everything trickles to the surface. Vogel stares at the documents, saturated with abandoned words and stranded numbers. Distinctions in this weak light are bleached. Words leak; numbers fade. Only spent clues remain: CMCTB, 3363/7014 ... flotsam on an opaque surface, wreckage after the deluge. In the milky gleam of a single bulb the heaped records look sapped, flaccid and lifeless.

Nineteen

"Dr. Vogel!"

There was a rat-tat-tat at the door, more urgent than the rhythm of ceaseless rain. "Hey, I know you're there, man - I can see the light. It's me, Nxumalo, your friend. It's pissing cows and goats out here. Let me in, Doc, I've got something to tell you!" The knocking rose to an insistent pummel and Vogel watched as minuscule peels of green paint sprinkled to the floor.

"Don't be stubborn, man. Do yourself a favour. This is crazy. You talking to those damn files? Wake up, Vogel! We've got stuff to discuss."

Lieutenant Nxumalo continued hammering on the door for another three minutes. He was yelling to make himself heard above the repetitive cadence of rainfall. Vogel could hear the lieutenant was becoming angry. Finally Nxumalo kicked the ill-fitting door with his army boots, dislodging another shower of paint shards onto the splintery floorboards.

As Vogel glanced down at the floor he saw a folded scrap of white paper. He picked it up. Had Nxumalo just slipped this under the door or had it been there when he had first entered and he simply hadn't noticed? Vogel unfolded the note. There was a scrawled biro message in disjointed capital letters: "Call Dep. Min. Biyela urgent", followed by a cell phone number.

'Files have a life of their own.' The words, said jokingly to Biyela, now mocked Vogel. Was this something Boschard had remembered from the time his agents had been spying on him years ago: or could this be a product of more recent surveillance? What had Boschard meant; what had he been trying to tell him? The archivist stared at the muddled heaps of documents.

Dossiers lay piled upon one another, ponderous and oppressive in their inert, collective mass, exuding a weak aroma of mulchy decay. How could he have ever imagined there was really life in these stagnant archives? The archivist had dreamed that the information, data, narratives and collective intelligence stored there could somehow cross-pollinate. He had thought of police agents and even researchers and archivists like himself as being the unconscious catalysts of this secret and mysterious migration of information. They spent their working lives comparing and transferring details from one file to another, like bees pollinating plants, or birds carrying seeds across frontiers and continents, so that one small kernel dropped - even inadvertently - on alien soil could fertilize a whole new cycle of information.

But as Vogel contemplated the damp disarray of files he felt that all remaining force had leaked out of them, and that the information had oozed instead into his own bloodstream and identity. The result was that rumours and toxins had seeped from the moldering records into his own soul.

Nothing remained fixed. The massive bulk of the mountain disintegrated and crumbled, worn away over millennia by wind and storms. Everything decomposed, especially under this pitiless monsoon. Damp slunk into every cleft, rotting fabric and turning the paper stored around him limp, yellow and mildewed. Ink in distinctive handwritten entries began to smudge. The black precision of official type-writers and uniform anonymity of computer print-outs fade and blanch, too. Memory and significance inexorably seep out of each sentence, until complete paragraphs decline into incoherence, and the individual words themselves eventually leak into unconsciousness. There appeared to be no words left here that could help Vogel make sense of himself. Even those that had thrown him into such turmoil would soon be gone, worn away by moisture and neglect. Time - hours, years - also seemed to dissolve under this harsh assault of wind and rain. Once the world, his world, had appeared obvious: the heroes and villains, black or white. Now in this ambiguous half-light of winter the logic of his own identity steadily dissolved as well, eroded by an oxidizing trickle of time, doubt and forgetfulness.

Why had the authorities not used that information on him in the files?

Had Vogel in fact, unknowingly, been useful to them … had he inadvertently betrayed his own friends? Words had always been the archivist's credo, an article of faith: that if only he could categorize words in the right order, all would become clear and be revealed. Now, surrounded by this immensity of sodden words, they threatened to erase him unhurriedly.

There were no words here to help him anymore. He would not find himself in these files. Instead there were people, today, who believed that he could have been an informer. Not just Boschard. Rafik and Lenny had also sensed such a possibility in him. That is not how he had seen himself. Yet others, friends, had discerned this potential of betrayal. And if the archivist could doubt, even suspect, Marda, then what … what did that make him?

It was still raining when he unlocked his door in the mid-afternoon. The archivist looked both ways to ensure there was no one in sight. Puddles on the rampart had united into a uniform shallow lagoon. To the west, out at sea, the gargantuan dark huff of cloud had parted, filtering a silver frown of thin sunlight over the sodden city.

Vogel weaved briskly between massed ranks of cars parked in the Grand Parade. Beggars, street children and illegal car attendants had all vanished. Vendors had dismantled their stalls and departed. City Hall looked forsaken; the buff yellow Bath limestone streaked and despondent, like a ruin from a lapsed civilization. It was days since he had been to the flower market. All the flower sellers were there, sitting patiently by unsold sprays and garlands. Rain drilled metrically on the sheet metal canopy of the arcade. Vogel was the sole customer and several women, wrapped in shawls and make-shift plastic waterproofs, called out to him.

"Hey, handsome, how's about some pretty lilies for your wife?"

"Sir, you always buy from me! My lilies was picked only now now."

Vogel realized that though he had been buying flowers here for over twenty years, frequently from the same women, some now grown old, he didn't know their names. Or if he ever had known, he'd forgotten. Contritely, from an elderly woman that he recognised, he bought two enormous armfuls of moist and creamy arum lilies. She beamed at him with no teeth.

"Those is your favourites, I know. Every time it's only the best, hey?"

In Adderley Street there were few pedestrians, but Vogel had to pay attention as people hurried straight towards him, rendered sightless and inattentive under umbrellas. Christmas decorations, still on display six months after their December summer dazzle, sagged across the rain-spattered street, unlit and doomed to displaced futility. Vogel, a bouquet of lilies in each arm, was drenched. He didn't care. He felt anesthetized. He waited on the corner of Bureau Street, opposite the Slave Lodge, obeying the red pedestrian traffic signal even though there was no traffic. Shouts and yells from the protesters in Spin Street were angrier and more forceful.

"The bones have risen."

"The bones have spoken."

Impulsively Vogel turned left. He strode towards the crowd. Despite the pitiless rain this assembly was now so large that it blocked off the whole of Spin Street. They were shouting at the lines of helmeted police, two-deep, which cordoned off the construction site.

Vogel marched straight towards this congregation. At the fringes of the gathering people ceased chanting and stepped aside to let him through. They glared at the bouquets of milky lilies in each arm. He heard hoarse murmurs, "White trash" … "Slave master." At the centre of the throng he saw Marc Hendricks, facing the police, a megaphone raised to his mouth. Sensing the crowd growing hushed, Hendricks turned. Vogel pushed on through the multitude, staring ahead. The crowd had fallen silent and as the archivist reached the far edge he heard a rasping voice through the megaphone, "Turncoat! Traitor!" A man spat at him.

The crowd had begun to boo. A young woman kicked him violently on both shins. Without changing pace, Vogel turned right into Plein Street, towards the mountain, partly obscured by rain and mist. Behind, catcalls and yells of fury swelled, and the hatred that he could hear filled his heart.

The echo of the megaphone followed him, "Sell out! Scab! Spy!"

Vogel recognized the revulsion of the crowd. He welcomed it and embraced the loathing. The yells followed him down the street. "Traitor, traitor." It was a relief to hear the words. The yells of disgust soothed him; they brought release. This excoriation was, at last, confirmation. The cry was taken up, repeated, and he could hear the howls of rage reverberating long minutes after he had vanished from view, even when he turned into the gutter-flooded, silent Sabata Dalindyebo Way and stood before his own front door. "Deserter, traitor ... spy." It was the cacophony of his own self-disgust.

The photograph was the only thing that remained unchanged. The young woman gazed back at him. It was exactly as he had remembered her.

Vogel laid both bouquets of lilies on the sideboard, one on either side of the black and white snapshot. In the gloom of his living room, despite the permanently closed curtains, her features were precise and engraved, fixed forever; yet when he looked away for a moment the memory dissolved.

He dropped to his knees before the photograph, grasping the silver frame in both hands and gazed fiercely at the venerated image, trying to fix it forever on his mind. His body shuddered with emotion. He whimpered. Tears, however, had evaporated. Only dry grits irritated his eyes. Marda's features, as soon as he turned away, blanched and dissolved beyond recall.

Twenty

VOGEL awoke to a serenely sunlit winter morning.

Mechanically he set off for work. Puddles were drying fast. He was about to cross into the public gardens when he realized the usual weekday grumble of traffic was absent and there were no cars on the road. Then he remembered it was a public holiday: commemoration of an uprising nearly three decades ago, the significance of which was now frequently forgotten. Instead the day was mostly enjoyed as one of liberty from work and routine.

The archivist turned and walked back into the warren of asymmetrical streets that mapped out his neighbourhood. The sun was warm on his face. He walked steadily, unwilling to return to his darkened and chilly home. He wandered down Vrede, Wandel, Gordon, Scott and Wesley. Normally such a detour through the archeology of his life and the nostalgic co-ordinates of his childhood would bring Vogel pleasure. He felt nothing. His legs ached. Walking was an effort. He didn't know what else to do. He didn't want to remain still. Yet walking seemed as though he was forcing his spent bones to go through the mechanical motions. Wherever he looked, images of death beckoned. This was not something he thought about or willed. Visions of his own carcass inexplicably materialized. He was trudging the pavement of Hope Street when a lone car raced in the opposite direction; as it passed, the archivist imagined his body falling under its wheels. Outside the Ladies Christian Home three young men sat on the steps, sunning themselves. As Vogel drew abreast he pictured the youths surrounding him and wordlessly pressing a blade into his side. Turning into Barnet Street he stepped over the broken shards of a beer bottle and glancing up he caught the momentary sight of his limp corpse slumped over coiled razor wire on a high brick wall.

It had begun that morning while shaving. Vogel dipped his razor into the basin and - without warning - imagined an oozing overflow of blood. He had not summoned this, or even thought it: the image simply appeared before his eyes and, with it, came a curious sensation of relief and peace.

Eventually Vogel turned south along Buitenkant. Toiling uphill he could see, over the high wall, the fluted teak columns and Corinthian crests of the sumptuous Dutch colonial mansion *Rust en Vreugd*. He followed the apricot-tinted wall round into Glynn Street, where on the opposite side a tall, shiny new silver wire fence cordoned off an empty car park.

Washing hung along the fence and plastic shopping bags dangled like bunting the length of the razor wire. A skeletal, almond-brown older man, stripped to the waist, was sprawled on the pavement, soaking up the winter sun. Indifferently he called out, "Give us some money, Mister."

Vogel hurried on. The man staggered to his feet, suddenly furious at being ignored, his tattered grey trousers almost falling off his emaciated shanks. "Listen," he yelled. "I'm accused number two! An' who the fuck you think you is, whitey?"

Vogel felt sluggish, flat. It was as though he had been unplugged, or a battery had run out. As if he were dragging a dead weight around, drained and pasty, mere carrion, not his own, something extraneous to him, an encumbrance: a cadaver. Everywhere he looked death beckoned enticingly.

As the archivist neared home, crossing the cobbles of Dunkley Square, there was a reverberating explosion, catapulting doves into the air from nearby trees and roofs. Vogel assumed the detonation was the noon-day cannon, fired from Signal Hill. Instinctively he checked his watch. It was only ten to twelve. The startled doves, with an agitated quiver of wings, looped the square before returning to their perches. The empty square was shadowless and silent. The only sound Vogel heard was his own footsteps.

As he turned the corner into Sabata Dalindyebo Way he saw someone stooping by his front door, as if spying through the keyhole.

"Oi!' bellowed Vogel and began running. The man twisted round. "Stop thief," yelled Vogel as the stranger took to his heels with an electric burst of speed. He had vanished before Vogel even reached his front door, badly winded by the sudden exertion and shock.

There was little the archivist could remember about the man, except that he was powerfully built, shaven-headed and black. Spontaneously a name surfaced in his mind: Mxolisi Mkapta. For a moment Vogel couldn't place this person. Then he remembered: Mkapta was the operative in the three-piece worsted suit that he'd met briefly in Boschard's office. Mxolisi Mkapta? Probably not, thought Vogel; this man today had seemed younger, wearing smart navy blue jeans, a matching crisp jeans jacket and immaculate white running shoes. But once again, uneasily, Vogel wondered if Boschard was working for Deputy Minister Biyela.

As he recovered, bent over, struggling to regain his breath, Vogel noticed there was a messy implosion of dark bird feathers strewn over the pavement. He glanced round. A plump pigeon lay splayed out in the gutter, dead, while further down the street, as if hobbling after the vanished prowler, another pigeon hopped and gyrated, shuddering, unable to take off. Quickly Vogel took out his keys and almost stepped on a third pigeon in his doorway: serenely still, almost unruffled, except for a dribble of blood from the jagged neck, which appeared to be scorched, while the head was nowhere to be seen.

Shaken, Vogel entered his darkened house, momentarily blinded after the harsh midday glare outside. In the gloom he noticed the red light of the answer phone flashing like an urgent semaphore. He pressed the play button automatically. The first message was curt: "D.K. Biyela here. It's imperative that I speak with you, Vogel. Call me. Only on my cell phone, thank you." Biyela left a number; then after a hiatus, as an afterthought, added, "Please."

The rest of the tape was full but there were no messages. Instead, after the end of each ring tone, there was a prolonged silence, then the caller hung up. Vogel listened to all twenty silences with implacably escalating unease.

A sliver of sunlight cut across the shadowed room. In his agitation, Vogel realized, he had forgotten to shut the door properly. He was about to close it when he spotted a postcard lying on the threshold that must have been pushed under the door while he was out. He picked it up and in the light from outside saw that the garish photograph on the front was the classic picture-postcard view of Cape Town, from across the bay, exactly as if it had been taken from the Xaba's flat. Vogel flipped the card over. Here, at least, was a message. Each letter had been cut carefully from newspaper headlines, and then pasted in sequence, exactly like his own black petals, to form three plain words in bold black type: BACK OFF WHITEBOY.

Twenty-one

The next morning Vogel rose late. He shaved. He walked to work. He submitted to habit. One day seemed much like another. It was a crisp, shimmering morning. There was a school tour of black and white and Indian teenage girls in the Castle courtyard and Vogel gazed vacantly at them, bewildered by their unfocused exuberance.

He hauled himself up the stone steps. On the parapet, the archivist saw a cluster of soldiers and civilians assembled outside the door next to his office. Vogel averted his eyes and hurriedly took out his keys to unlock his own identical green door.

"Dr. Vogel!"

Lieutenant Nxumalo sauntered across, hands in his pockets.

"We've been talking about you." Nxumalo smiled benignly as he waited for a reaction from the archivist. "We were wondering, in fact, if you'd finally show up today."

Nxumalo shrugged when Vogel did not reply. "Regrettably, you are missing all the excitement, Dr. Vogel." He had moved into Vogel's path, blocking him from his office door. "After the public disorders yesterday, you see, Deputy Minister D.K. Biyela instructed that the slave bones from Spin Street be transported here, for safekeeping. They were excavating all night. The bones arrived at the Castle early this morning - a whole truck load. And they're stored here, next to your office. Hundreds of bones packed in crates. Kinda spooky, huh? Right up to the ceiling. Like your files, Dr. Vogel."

The archivist tried to manoeuvre round the lieutenant but Nxumalo put out a restraining hand. With his other arm, he indicated the group gathered outside the adjacent door. "Of course, you know Mr. Hendricks, convener of the Slave Commemoration Committee," continued Nxumalo cheerfully. "Mr. Hendricks and I are now responsible for the security of the skeletons until a decision has been taken about what to do with them."

Marc Hendricks stood to one side of the group, flanked by the two identically-suited, shaven-headed men that Vogel had seen outside the Hendricks' home some weeks before. They stared at Vogel indifferently.

"That's right, a truce has been negotiated, you see," said Nxumalo. "There will be a joint guard outside this storeroom - half soldiers, half from the Slave Committee. It's a compromise that will allow the bones to be protected - around the clock." The lieutenant chuckled. "Might be good news for you, too, y'know ... I mean, should anyone be tempted to break into your store-room, and take a look at those precious files, eh?"

The archivist tried to move past Nxumalo again but the soldier tightened his grip.

"Our instructions from Minister Biyela is that no one, not even the Castle Commandant, is allowed in with those old remains." The lieutenant released his grip. "But I'm sure we could make an exception ... especially for a friend of Mr. Hendricks. Wouldn't you like to see those famous bones, Dr. Vogel? Check out the actual relics which are causing all this fuss?"

The archivist pressed past Nxumalo and, his back shielding him from onlookers, fiddled nervously with his batch of keys for nearly a minute before he found the right one.

Nxumalo called, "Dr. Vogel, you hear about the bomb yesterday morning?"

Vogel unlocked his door. Before closing it behind him, he glanced back swiftly. Marc Hendricks was watching impassively.

Hendricks shrugged. "The bones have spoken."

Vogel sat in his office. Outside he could hear a low mutter of voices. He was shaken. He was unable to concentrate. He became increasingly apprehensive. He didn't know why. At intervals, for no reason and without warning, he felt frightened. His stomach ached. Vogel felt precipitously nauseous. These fits would last for up to twenty minutes then suddenly pass, leaving him with a residue of undefined terror. He stared at the files. They looked as lifeless to him as stacked crates of skeletons. At last absolutely everything, it appeared, had risen to the surface - yet still revealed nothing.

The idea that files might have a life of their own now seemed insane. These files were not only lifeless, they were rotting and disintegrating. The archivist was embarrassed to recall his thought that documents, like trees, might possess their own imperceptible code of communication. The reason mopane trees didn't have a permanent defense against browsers, he realised, was that if they constantly produced tannin to make their leaves too bitter to eat, they'd end up by poisoning themselves. Vogel wondered if he had polluted himself. The fact he was perpetually on the defensive - above all, that he'd buried his feelings about Marda for twenty-five years - could well have spread bitter toxins throughout his system until it affected his mind.

The archivist felt repelled by the files. They seemed altogether alien to him, as strange and inaccessible as the Dead Sea scrolls. These archives, Vogel reflected, might as well be a decayed collection of unknown human remains, desiccated bones: skeletons of nameless people from centuries ago, forgotten and anonymous, erased from memory.

As Vogel surveyed the dusty, airless, file-packed store-room, he was reminded of the parting sally as he had turned to leave Boschard's office. It was as though Boschard had entered not only his thoughts and feelings but his work habits as well. How could he know to what shrunken confines the archivist's life had dwindled unless he were keeping him under surveillance? Perhaps Lieutenant Nxumalo, Vogel reflected dully, was his spy. "Yes, you and the late Signor Pessoa have much in common." Boschard's calm voice sounded disconcertingly close, as if he were lurking behind the stacked files. "*Only in the dead air of closed rooms do I breathe the normality of my life.*"

He didn't turn on the light and his office was pitch black by the time Vogel realized that he could no longer hear voices outside. Warily he opened the door. By the light of a waxen half-moon he saw there were only two men guarding the next room; one soldier and a civilian. Hastily he locked his door and without a word, scurried past them.

Pastel moonlight cast a haunting albino glaze over the Grand

157

Parade. The car park was desolate. Street children huddled over the blaze of a fire by the statue of Edward VII. Spin Street was silent. The crowds had evaporated. Only a pair of armed policemen lurked in the dark, guarding the ghostly, fenced-off construction site. Seized by unreasoning panic, Vogel increased his pace, trying not to run, until he reached Sabata Dalindyebo Way. The archivist paused, breathless, outside his front door.

A fresh ocean breeze ruffled down the street and Vogel noticed his thick, draped curtains quiver. He watched them shiver before the puffs of wind. It took him a moment to realize that the curtains were fluttering because the window was open. The lower section of the sash window had been raised to its full extent, sufficient to allow someone to clamber through. He never opened this window, just as he hardly ever drew the living-room curtains. Hastily he checked if there were any marks on the frame to indicate that the window had been forced. In the dark, he could see nothing.

All his neighbours had burglar bars and alarms. Vogel had resisted such precautions on the vague assumption that having lived there his entire life he would somehow be immune from common break-ins. Fumbling, and trying to be as quiet as possible, he unlocked the door. Pausing to listen for a moment, he snapped on the light. The room was untouched, exactly as it had been for twenty-five years. Only the curtains shivered uneasily. Marda's photograph was in its customary place. He noticed the white blooms of the lilies on each side of the framed picture were fading to brown at the edges.

Lightheaded with terror and shock, the archivist raced upstairs. He flicked on the light switch in his study. Nothing appeared to have been disturbed. Vogel strode to the bookcase, heart thumping. A fortnight before, prompted by old habits and precautions, he had removed the two police files from the drawer of his desk and hidden them in the bookcase, inside his student copy of *The Archivist's Handbook*. Both folders were exactly where he'd placed them. Vogel opened the files, green and beige, flicking through the red-lined pages of official reports. The dossiers were obviously intact. The history of his clandestine life - the surveillance, the concealment, the gossip and conjecture - remained undisclosed, overlooked: still his secret.

Vogel proceeded methodically through the house. He could find nothing missing. He closed the window and latched it. Could he have opened the window absent-mindedly that morning? Such an action would be altogether out of character. But then, he reflected, both his routine and disposition had been drastically dislocated recently.

The archivist wandered restlessly from room to room, each time expecting to discover signs of disturbance. He would have to follow his neighbours' example, he reflected: burglar bars, grilled gates, security alarms and beams, even possibly razor wire on the railings of his balcony.

The thought of iron bars made him feel hemmed in. Vogel was unable to sleep. Was he paranoid, he fretted; or was he, once again, under scrutiny?

Twenty-two

BY dawn the archivist had resolved for his own safety or sanity to return both files. He set out at six thirty with the two dossiers tucked into his duffel bag. En route to work, however, all the archivist noticed - on private homes, shops, schools, office buildings, in fact wherever he looked - were security bars, grilled metal gates and high walls, vicious spikes, razor wire and surveillance cameras; like a city under siege.

Alongside this ubiquitous modern armory, the broad stone battlements of the 17th century Castle blended in, curiously timeless. There were only two people outside the bone storeroom at this early hour, Lieutenant Nxumalo and Marc Hendricks. They stopped talking. Vogel ignored them.

"You know," remarked Nxumalo conversationally, "I should really search you, Dr. Vogel. Check what you've got in that bag. This is a high security area now, see."

"I'm hardly likely to be smuggling confidential material in, Lieutenant," snapped Vogel. "You can search me when I leave."

Nxumalo and Hendricks exchanged glances.

Nxumalo sighed. "Just kidding, comrade. However, I should warn you, Dr. Vogel, that there may be more bones shipped over from Spin Street later today - in which case, we might have to commandeer your office, too."

Vogel immediately turned round and walked away fast. He followed his customary route back to Sabata Dalindyebo Way. Once home, he locked and bolted his front door, then hurried upstairs to slip both files back into their hiding place in *The Archivist's Handbook*. Vogel was completely disoriented. He had lost all routine. He didn't know what to do.

He fell asleep in front of the TV. When he woke it was dark. He heard his phone ring. There had been several messages during the week: a couple from Zechariah and Mary, to which he had not replied, and at least five from D.K. Biyela, the Minister's irritation giving way to barely concealed displeasure with each successive unreturned call.

This message, however, was from Sivuyile Gqabe. "Return my calls, bru. What do I have to do ... beg? There's profit in it for you, too, comrade. Things are getting out of hand. I need your help, *Bhuti*. You're the only one everyone trusts."

Vogel was bewildered. What did Sivu mean: he was the only one everyone trusted? He no longer even trusted himself. He retreated to bed. Only sleep brought relief. When he woke it was late Saturday afternoon.

Sivuyile had left two further messages. Both repeated the same thing: "Macaulay, please. You are the only one everyone trusts."

There was also another message from the Deputy Minister. His tone was brusque. "Vogel, what the hell are you playing at? You know who this is. We need to speak. Now, urgently. Stop screwing me around, Vogel. This is an order! You have my cell number. Call immediately."

He had neither the energy nor will to respond. He felt energy leaking away. The structure of his life was dissolving. The sense of himself was dissolving. Time dissolved; minutes crawled by slowly, hours endlessly.

The monthly Sunday ascent of Table Mountain had always given him a profound sense of perspective, routine and companionship. Would tomorrow, Vogel tried to recall, have been their scheduled Sunday? Perhaps Edwin and Rafik also missed the camaraderie.

He called Susan. "Don't call," she remarked casually and hung up.

He rang Rafik, "Hey ..." but Rafik didn't even bother to speak before replacing the receiver.

Vogel lay on the bed with his clothes on, staring at the shadowy ceiling. He hadn't bothered to turn on any lights. Overwhelming lassitude trickled over him and he seeped into unconsciousness. It was dark and icy when he woke on Sunday evening.

The archivist left the darkened house hurriedly. He walked swiftly, with purpose. He crossed the hushed, dim-lit streets of his childhood.

Soon he was striding east through the bulldozed desolation of District Six. Once there had been crowded alleyways and noisy tenements on this weed-strewn wasteland: a green scar gouged on his memory. Vogel turned abruptly south where he had known a steep cobbled lane, and he climbed the grassy incline as if mounting those remembered, ghostly steps. Arctic wind blew in from the sea; then he, too, was rapidly enveloped by the vast black petal of the night.

Twenty-three

THE only light was a tawny nightglow from the city below. Though Vogel had no purpose or objective beyond driving himself higher into the dark and pitiless cold, he strode stubbornly up the darkened gravel track of Devil's Peak. He stumbled, fell several times, grating the palms of his hands.

He left the jeep track and cut blindly across vaporous pine plantations. Climbing alone, at night, with no food or water and without any protective clothing, violated every tenet of mountain lore. Each season the mountain claimed fresh victims, too foolish to fear its unpredictable metabolism of abrupt mists, malevolent cloudbursts, or at night the deathly chill.

To reach this path, Vogel had needed to cross the silent motorway.

Just as he reached the verge of the M3, he heard a sound behind him. He turned but could see nothing. Then as he was about to cross, he imagined he heard voices and looked again. At the outer edge of a sinister yellow glow of street lamps he saw three or four indistinct figures, blurry, like shadows in a fog. They seemed to be moving in his direction. Had he been followed? It occurred to him that they might even be connected to all those silent messages on his answer phone or that belligerent warning on the postcard.

Instantly, irrationally, Vogel thought of Mr. Mxolisi Mkapta, his vigorously muscled frame compressed tightly into that incongruous three-piece worsted suit. What if Mkapta had been called into Boschard's office only moments before his own entrance; summoned solely in order to permit the brawny investigator to obtain a close personal look at Boschard's unexpected visitor?

This, the archivist realized, would be a perfect spot to deal with him.

Vogel looked around for somewhere to hide. Behind him he heard a shrill shout. No, more likely these phantoms were simply loitering muggers waiting for an incautious nocturnal stroller so that they could steal his wallet. They'd certainly assume that someone who looked like him would carry a cell phone. He'd heard and read about plenty of late night stabbings for the sake of a few bucks or even a pair of shoes. Abruptly he was assailed by a blizzard of panic: a long suppressed horror, stoked up by endless rumor and reports of unbridled butchery - about feral street children, psychotic teenage drug addicts or casually violent gangsters.

Vogel broke into a sprint across the M3 motorway. He was breathless with fright rather than exertion. His legs appeared leaden. They seemed to move excruciatingly slowly. It felt as if he were barely advancing and Vogel was gripped, almost paralysed, by an overwhelming terror. He was certain that he would never make it to the other side of the motorway alive. A lone, low-slung car with only one crazily angled headlight veered round the bend and accelerated towards him, racing straight into the path of his escape route. With its skewed headlight, Vogel realised that the driver probably hadn't yet spotted him and he hurled himself to the ground, skidding along the tarmac, carried along by the momentum of his terrified dash.

The car sped past, missing his arms and legs by centimeters, fanning Vogel's face with the suction of its velocity. He heard a blast of harsh male laughter and thumping music like a mobile disco. Then the rust-gouged car vanished downhill towards the silent, sleeping city. The archivist rose with difficulty. Though the motorway was completely deserted again, he could still hear a receding beat from the amplified sound system.

His knees were bruised and throbbing; hands scraped raw and stinging. Vogel noticed his right palm was speckled with droplets of blood where the uneven tarmac had sandpapered his skin, leaving pale, delicate strips of flesh fluttering painfully in the wind. Quickly Vogel glanced back and saw that he was alone, stranded on the motorway. He peered down the incline below him and in the hazy yellow lamplight Vogel observed that the group he had imagined were pursuing him had not moved. Now he could make out that there were three of them. They were children, probably no more than eleven or twelve years old he guessed. One was pointing at him while the others made exaggeratedly obscene gestures. All three were laughing manically. The wind wafted up the wild cackle of their derision. Disconsolately Vogel pictured himself as they must perceive him: an absurd and petrified middle-aged gent, spooked by a trio of undernourished kids who hadn't even moved.

He hobbled to the far side of the motorway, humiliated and ashamed, close to tears. Stiffly he began to clamber up the steep and densely tufted embankment and began his long, solitary climb up the dark mountainside.

His hands were lacerated and throbbing but before long he was indifferent. He grew oblivious to the shiver of scouring ocean-soaked gusts. He rejoined the jeep track, then found a rough footpath and doggedly began a twisting ascent. Vogel kept his eyes down, watching only his feet.

He walked for hours. He lost sense of time. He could hear a desperate, arduous breathing, a sound that seemed extraneous to him like the fading pants of a wounded animal, uneven and worn out, as though a dying beast were tracking him out there in the skulking night. He observed his feet crunching over the gravel path, aware only of the instant.

Vogel felt like a man with no past, no future.

Indifferently he passed through stubby foliage, stony outcrops and open meadows. The path took a sharp turn and Vogel tripped on a fallen branch. He tumbled to the moist earth. Twisting round to regain his feet, the archivist saw that the cloud cover overhead had cleared. The night sparkled with moonlit, icy beauty. Out to sea, westward, extending the entire length of the horizon was a fleecy mountain of curdled fog, appearing to steam out of the dark Atlantic.

Vogel sat on the uneven path, transfixed by the thought that spread out before him was the landscape runaway slaves would have seen. Now a dazzling constellation of electric lights illuminated the nocturnal city and multiplied luminously across what had then been a sandy wasteland. He could make out the curve of the bay and the murky hump of Robben Island. This constricted panorama, lit up, mapped out the entire compass of his life.

As Vogel tried to identify individual streets and personal landmarks, bewildering memories surfaced. Searching for Sabata Dalindyebo Way, he unexpectedly imagined his mother posing outside their home in Yonge Street, beaming proudly. Tracing the line of Adderley Street down to the docks, Vogel remembered the roasting afternoon when he'd seen his brother Michael off on that sea voyage to Europe from which he would never return.

For over thirty years he'd expunged that painful day from his thoughts. Now, without warning, Vogel recalled - exactly - the moment that the stately Union Castle liner eased away from the dock. He had boiled with resentment. Watching the ship slowly recede from Cape Town, Macaulay Vogel had felt irrevocably that his elder brother was, henceforth, dead to him. Forever.

He had despised Michael for openly pretending to be white, despite the fact that this had always been Nadira's expressed hope and exhortation. The archivist experienced a discomforting, tender shock of pity for his older brother. Michael, in truth, had only acted out the very same deception which Vogel himself had allowed by default. The difference, he reflected, was that Michael, being several years older, had known everything.

Michael had been condemned to remember.

He had been unable, unlike Vogel, to wipe out the memory of their early years at the mission station. He had been unable, unlike Vogel, to blot out the memory of those loud, brutal quarrels about their names. Principally, Michael had been unable to suppress the memory of that final, vicious fight after Gershon had discovered that, during his absence at sea, his younger son had never been baptised Isak at all, and that legally he had another name.

Vogel had simply evaded that part of his pain by eliminating it from his memory. Yet it was this very name, Macaulay, formally endorsed on all his documents, that conferred upon him an implicit European identity.

Michael, in contrast, had not only been registered with that irrefutable, tell-tale first name of Malek ... but because he'd been born before Nadira and Gershon were married, he'd also been burdened with their mother's maiden name. This, too, was on all his documents so that no matter what intricate lies Michael or his mother told later on, those baptismal names were always there on official documents, as brazen as a brand on his forehead.

That surname October was an unmistakable marker of slave ancestry: a rudimentary label bestowed by indifferent owners, assigning slaves to the time of year that they had been purchased, so stripping them of any earlier identity. Michael - Malek - had also looked far more like the slave Octobers. Macaulay, on the other hand, took after his much lighter-skinned father Gershon. So in the past, especially at university, whenever Vogel was asked about his family background he'd been able to mumble vaguely about Mediterranean antecedents ("Portuguese or Greek emigrants," he invariably claimed) marrying into Dutch-born Vogels.

Their mother's cunning, he now realized, was to publicly retain her married name after she'd separated from Gershon, thus disguising him in Cape Town under a surname - Vogel - which could as easily have been that of the slave as of a master. And Vogel had subsequently lived out that very ambiguity, deluding himself, he now recognized, as much as anyone else.

All the same, while Vogel had enjoyed the luxury of forgetfulness, he too had always instinctively sought the shadows: the camouflage of the State Archives; the anonymity of a doctorate by correspondence; then an illusory warranty thanks to that title, Dr. Vogel. Who had been the more deceiving?

From the police files Vogel had also learnt that his father's family had been Muslim. Was there anything at all about him now that was real or true?

The archivist became aware that for the first time in over thirty years he did not suffer the habitual acidic burn of rancour and aggression when he contemplated his older brother. Michael, Vogel now finally understood, had never once attempted to shift any of that corrosive gall of remembrance onto him. Poor Michael, poor Malek: no wonder he had sought to escape.

Vogel thought: in reviling Michael, I have only condemned myself.

As a teenager, it was from almost precisely this vantage point high on the mountain that Vogel, on that blazing afternoon, had witnessed the great Union Castle liner vanish forever. He had raced straight from the docks and by the time he'd scrabbled up this far, breathless, the mighty passenger ship was already a distant shimmer, a vanishing memory on the vastness of the alienating ocean. Vogel had no idea where his brother might be today, nor whether he were alive or dead, and he felt a sudden, unutterable sorrow: for Michael; for himself. He remembered how he had bawled with youthful rage as his brother, on that forlorn pilgrimage to Europe, finally evaporated into nothingness. It had been a clear, hot afternoon. Now as Vogel stared into the icy-clear night it was as though he were examining the negative imprint of a discolored black and white photo: a young man, alone on the mountainside, hurling frenzied accusations of betrayal and abandonment into the wind.

Out of the dark he imagined he heard a voice, "None of us have a past, Mac ... it was all made-up. There's no shared history except for the pain." It sounded exactly like Malek and Vogel looked around. There was no one. It had been his own voice, excessively loud in his head.

The night had grown sharply colder, but the air was crisp and fresh. He noticed silky white buds floating through the dark. They fluttered down, gently drifting, spinning playfully with the breeze: pretty white petals that glimmered crystalline against blackness.

It took him several seconds to realize that it had begun snowing.

Snow on the mountain!

This was so rare and improbable that Vogel felt like a remote observer gazing through a window - the panes blurred by snow flakes - on a familiar yet still unidentified landscape. With this impetuous flurry of movement and memory, barely for one ecstatic, fugitive moment, Macaulay Vogel thought that he saw an indistinct shape, a blanched face: thought he saw her passing, passing by; saw the image, hers, that wasn't now passing, wasn't passing by.

He shifted uncomfortably. His crossed legs were aching and cramped, his bruised knees were painfully stiff and inflamed, and the coarse gravel and stones on the pathway bit through his trousers into his buttocks. He became aware of the Arctic wind. He glanced at his watch. It was well past midnight. He must have been sitting in the dark on this path for over an hour.

He rose stiffly, all the grazes and discomfort from his fall on the motorway were throbbing, and as he dusted the gravel from his trousers an impulsive thought struck him: if you can forgive Michael, you can forgive yourself.

This reflection came to Vogel like a whisper. It was calm, tender and surprisingly cheerful: a familiar voice, long - far too long - unheard. Vogel sensed that Marda was present, a breathing presence, soothing, close to him.

The white petals had evaporated before reaching the ground. There were no more flakes in the air. It had stopped snowing. He was probably the only person in the entire city to have witnessed this wonderful, incomparable sight, so brief that it was like a dream. No one would believe him: snow on the mountain! Exactly like the first year that Europeans had arrived here on this distant and inaccessible tip of Africa in order to establish a settlement and, cruel timing, that very winter it had also snowed on Table Mountain.

How they must have regretted coming to Africa ... how intensely they must have longed to return home. How different everything might have been!

Vogel laughed out loud.

Sensation flooded back into his body and abruptly Vogel felt chilled. He was exhausted and hungry and thirsty. He felt grimy and chaffed. The cuts and abrasions on his hands throbbed again. The raw wind was piercing.

The archivist started back down the mountain path as fast as he could. Descending in the dark was hazardous, but he felt invigorated and, among the pines, broke into a run. By the time Vogel slid down the final short slope again and re-crossed the motorway, a glassy lilac dawn rinsed the horizon.

Early morning traffic was already backing up. At the intersection of Buitenkant and Roeland half a dozen hawkers weaved among the stationary cars, selling plastic coat hangers, ostrich feather dusters, carved wooden animals and improvised wire toys. A laughing youth in a luminous orange bib jogged past, carrying a hefty pile of newspapers.

He waved a copy of the *Cape Times* to entice the stalled drivers, yelling: "Victoria's head found!"

Vogel crossed the road as the news vendor raced by to make a sale.

"S'all here," he hollered. "Funnies, crime, glamour, sport ..."

On the front page, Vogel glimpsed a picture of Marc Hendricks and Sivuyile Gqabe. They were smiling and shaking hands, surrounded by a posse of beaming dignitaries, including the archdeacon and deputy mayor.

The archivist hurried home. He shaved and showered and changed his clothes. He removed the two security police files that he had concealed in his bookcase. Vogel was about to go out again when he saw the red light of his answer phone flashing in the heavily curtained gloom like a frantic SOS, signaling distress and danger. He hesitated, and instead noticed the identical pair of bouquets: limp, decomposing lilies on either side of Marda's portrait. He scooped up the blackened flowers and tossed them into the bin.

Twenty-four

IT was a buttery, winter-bright morning. The archivist drove round the arc of the bay to Bloubergstrand. There was a rising sea swell. Robben Island, ominous in the dark only hours before, emerged unruffled from choppy wavelets. Zechariah and Mary were astonished to see him.

"You haven't been returning our calls," admonished Zechariah.

"We were worried, love," added Mary. "Rumours are flying …"

Zechariah's face was so inflamed that he could only speak slowly and with difficulty. A livid crimson-bluish welt spread across the right side of his face. This bruise was so distended that one eye was almost closed, and on his garishly swollen lower lip a plaster barely covered a deep, jagged gash.

"I was mugged yesterday," explained Zechariah sheepishly. "Two young black youths, just boys actually, set upon me in broad daylight. They knocked me down from behind, slamming me into the pavement. One held me pinned to the ground, while the other held a knife to my throat and searched my pockets. I didn't even recognize what language they spoke. Fortunately I had some money in my wallet, otherwise I really think they would have slit my throat out of sheer rage and hatred."

"Zech, that's terrible. I mean, you … you of all people."

"Oh, the youth today - no respecters of one's colour anymore!"

"God, I'm so sorry. That's so unfair. Are you okay?"

"Anyway," added Zechariah with a pained, lopsided grin, "as these kids ran away, I staggered to my feet and yelled after them, 'I still support your revolutionary aspirations, my children!'"

"That's quite enough of that, thank you," interjected Mary sharply. "Come in, Mac."

173

There were chaotic piles of paper strewn over every surface of their living-room: stacked on chairs, over the couch and the oval table, as well as hundreds of pages scattered haphazardly across the bare wooden floor. Vogel had to step carefully not to disturb them.

"The next issue of *Umhlobo*," explained Zechariah.

"We're hoping to distribute this Saturday, at the latest on Sunday," specified Mary. "Things are hotting up, Mac. People are incredibly jumpy right now - especially after Queen Victoria was blown up."

"Victoria was ... what?"

"Jeez, where've the hell you been this past week?"

"You must've heard the explosion," scolded Zechariah. "How could you miss such drama? You're buried in those archives, Macaulay. With a statue blown up right outside Parliament, Deputy Minister Biyela is now claiming this attack constitutes a direct assault on the state."

"Police are out in force. Army road blocks in the townships, too."

"It was a professional job," observed Zechariah with an expert's appreciation. "Exactly enough explosive to blow apart the body, with no damage at all to Victoria's head."

"That's right. Because on Saturday night, her marble royal *kop* ..."

"Was hurled right through the glass entrance of the corporation trying to build that fancy hotel in Spin Street, where the bones were uncovered."

"I see," said Vogel. He nodded ruefully. "I should have guessed."

He surveyed the chaos, a scramble of pages so random it was hard to imagine they could ever be brought to order. Unlike himself, he reflected, Zechariah - despite having been tortured - maintained a cheerful confidence in the potential of everyone, allied to an undimmed passion that only the truth, exposed to all, could finally set them free. That's why Zechariah and Mary produced *Umhlobo* intermittently, with their own money. Zech was like a priest, thought Vogel, who had lost his formal faith but never a belief in people. Perhaps it was Mary's name, the same as the selfless wife of the evangelical explorer Dr. Livingstone, which sometimes made the archivist think of them as akin to a nineteenth century missionary couple, united against seemingly irreversible odds. Livingstone, in all his years in Africa, only ever made one convert - and Sechele, a Bechuana chief, later recanted. Vogel was convinced, whatever the reversals or recantations of others, that Zechariah and Mary remained steadfast. He trusted them unconditionally.

"Here," he said. "My security police files."

"Mac, you were supposed to put them back in the archives!"

"Don't worry. I made photocopies of both of them on my way over." Vogel reached into his duffel bag. "See, here are the originals. I'll take them back tomorrow and place them safely among all the other files. No one will ever know I smuggled them out, I promise. And here are the photocopies."

He handed one set, which he took out of the scruffy lime green folder, to Zechariah; the other, from the beige folder, to Mary. "I'd like you to keep these copies for me."

Zechariah replied, "We have plenty of hiding places, believe me."

"Old habits," laughed Mary. "Don't worry, they'll be safe with us."

"I have another request," added Vogel impulsively.

"Anything, Mac."

"You only have to ask, love."

"I'd like you both to read them."

Zechariah and Mary glanced at each other uneasily.

"Oh no," replied Mary. "I don't think so, really."

"But ..."

"Some things should stay private, Mac," interrupted Zechariah.

"But you don't know who I am!"

"We know, love. We know exactly."

"No you don't," insisted Vogel. "There are things about me that ..."

"That should remain closed in this file," concluded Zechariah firmly.

"You don't even know my real name." Vogel looked from one to the other imploringly. "I need you to know. About me, my family. It's all there. I'm not who you think I am, you see."

Mary said, "What we need to know can't possibly be in any file."

"We'll keep those photocopies out of harm's way, though," confirmed Zechariah. "Laid to rest, forever."

"But they won't stay buried," corrected Vogel. "It's like the bones, you see. One day, they'll just work their own way to the surface."

"Well, let's wait till that day comes, love. After all, they've even managed to arrive at a compromise over those damn bones."

"Oh yeah?" muttered Vogel sourly.

"Uh-huh, it's all in the *Times* today," Zechariah told him. "They've agreed to build a state-of-the-art memorial at the corner of Spin Street."

"The American corporation will pay, of course," added Mary. "In return, Marc Hendricks has agreed the bones can finally be scientifically tested, while construction on the hotel will continue immediately."

"And Marc?"

"Chairman of a new Slave Trust, funded by the corporation. It's a big deal, Mac. There'll be a ritzy Foundation, symposiums and conferences."

"I see," said Vogel. "Well, they both got what they wanted, I guess."

"Still, you mustn't compare the bones to your files, love. Whoever they belonged to, those bones were once people. Breathing, living souls. I mean, I know you care passionately about your archives, Mac, but let's face it - they're just things. Dead objects, totally lifeless."

"Mary, they're not inanimate. In their effects, at any rate. All that stuff, that info? It trickles out, in the end. Files have a life of their own, you see."

"They're only pieces of paper, for God's sake!"

"But the infection's already seeped out, Mary, and it's poisoning practically everyone. Just add up the score so far. Edwin's totally pissed off. Rafik hangs up immediately if I call. Susan Sarkissian won't speak to me. Grethe and Lenny are ... embarrassed. Even Boschard. Yeah, even the bloody cop in charge of our surveillance just wants me to shut up."

"Of course! Now do you see what we're up against?"

"*Bhuti*, there's a powerful coincidence of interests here. They don't mind you fossicking about among the records, sorting files, putting 'em in order, examining and classifying - just so long as it all remains archived."

"People don't want you raking up the past, love."

"Especially if unsavory details emerge."

"You make me feel a bit like those wild dogs that used to dig up corpses from the cemetery in Church Square."

Zechariah laughed. "That's exactly it, you're digging up dead bodies."

"But I haven't done anything! I only want to find out about myself."

"Join the queue, my brother," grimaced Zechariah. "I applied ages ago for access to my file. Wrote to everyone. The Ministry, the police, you name it. They all told me to talk to another department. In the end I was informed my file had to remain classified. So I went to see Deputy Minister Biyela."

"And?"

"Oh, D.K. was charming. We talked about old times, joked. But there was nothing he could do, he claimed. His hands were tied, those were his very words." Zechariah chuckled. "On one hand, he said that the constitution guarantees me freedom of information. At the same time, though, it assures others of the right to privacy. People who might have informed on me, say."

The archivist hesitated. "Okay," he beamed. "Then why don't I smuggle out some of the other files? There are departmental records for security cops, for example. We could start with those - like Colonel Boschard's!"

Zechariah and Mary were silent. Midday sun blazed through the window, illuminating the anarchy of papers strewn across the room.

Vogel said, "This is our chance. Don't you see? It's an opportunity at last to break the silence, and shine light into ..."

"They'd really gun for you then," objected Mary.

Zechariah sighed. "Biyela would be after you ... not just Boschard."

"Look, in the end, everything leaks anyway. As it is, it's only by keeping all those records and files in the dark that rumours circulate and people can still smear one another. Hell, I've come across a couple of politicians, senior government officials, a prominent academic, who all obviously ..."

"You're kidding? That's precisely what D.K. Biyela was warning you against - exposing influential people who were compromised in the past."

177

"Mac, that's when some very powerful people will really get mad."

"They'd hammer you," agreed Zechariah. "Too many people want that stuff kept under lock and key. In any case, old friend, you're supposed to be working under military regulations, remember. Prison would be the least of it. You'd be vilified as a turncoat yourself."

"Okay, but if I brought out one at a time, would you publish them?"

"Maybe." Zechariah grinned. "Maybe we could - I don't know - mix them up a bit. Make it look like the information came from several sources."

Mary interrupted to bustle them into the tiny kitchen for lunch, where she kept up a stream of distracting, lighthearted chatter. It was only much later, after they had returned to the cluttered living room, that Vogel found himself able to return at last to the subject that consumed him. Zechariah had been drinking whisky steadily all afternoon, and his swollen mouth seemed to have eased considerably and he was able to talk much more naturally than before. He heaved himself out of his armchair. "Wait, hold it right there," he ordered. "I must take a short break. Help yourself to a refill, ol' buddy."

Mary waited until he had padded down the corridor and she heard a door close. "Mac, don't pursue this, about publishing the files. Please don't tempt him, I beg you. If there was any trouble the person who would be first in the line of fire of course would be Zechariah." She placed a beseeching hand on Vogel's arm. "He's not in a good frame of mind at all. Oh, I know he appears so up and cheerful to you. But he's not always like that anymore, not when we're alone. He can get very, very angry. And it frightens me. He's disgusted with people like D.K. Biyela, the ones who drive humungous cars and parade around with squads of bodyguards. He's repelled by their excesses. It just mimics the inequalities we fought to end. Sure, Zech hides it well, but he's sickened, Mac. He agrees with our former comrade Jeremy, who's stayed the Party and in Parliament and sees some of these show-offs up close ... and, well, he reckons many of our nouveau blackoisie actually believe that by flaunting their riches they somehow embody the dreams of the poor. Wild, huh? That by virtue of their colour, with

178

such ostentatious consumption, they somehow symbolically represent the downtrodden and dispossessed in the marble halls of opulence!"

Before Vogel could reply, Mary added fiercely, "So I'm asking you, please, please, don't encourage him in this idiotic crusade. He's pissed off, Mac, and disillusioned and he's gone back to drinking far, far too much."

"Zech seems in good form to me," objected Vogel uncertainly. "I mean, apart from those nasty bruises and cuts from his mugging."

They heard the toilet flush and then a door open down the corridor. "But he wasn't mugged, you see," whispered Mary hurriedly. "That's just a good story to gloss over his embarrassment. Yesterday he'd been drinking all afternoon and then, in the dark, fell down the concrete stairwell outside."

Zechariah reappeared in the doorway, his puffy face creased by a hopelessly skewed grin. "Well, now I've got rid of that lot, I need some more soothing medication. Another whisky, Mac?" Zechariah had already filled two glasses to the brim. "I've been thinking about our old friend D.K. Biyela," he continued. "The Deputy Minister's a dangerously driven man. He's a nationalist, a populist. Who knows why he set you among those files. Maybe to discover if there was any compromising information he could use against others. Or to protect his own back? We need to be careful you're not being used in power struggles we don't even know about. He might also find it useful to single you out as a white scapegoat. My advice is, beware D.K."

"Yup, okay, I hear you," agreed Vogel. "All the same, Zech, if you'd actually managed to get hold of your file, what would you have done?"

"Published, of course!"

"Even if it was embarrassing for you?"

"We have to face the past, someday."

"Whatever the consequences?"

"Remember Mac, in Hebrew, Zechariah means 'Yahweh remembers.' Maybe it's a curse, not being able to forget. But, yes, despite everything ... whatever the consequences."

"Then," replied the archivist, "why not publish my files?"

"Because, Macaulay, they're classified documents. You could get into trouble. Serious trouble."

"But it's about me, only embarrassing to me. Humiliating, in fact."

"Not the point, love," interjected Mary. "Listen, I'm a lawyer. You'd go to jail - and for what? The bad guys would still be free."

"Do you really think they'd prosecute for what amounts to a public service? No, the worst thing would be the indignity of the whole world knowing about my love life. But there's lots of other stuff there. Reference numbers, codes. You must admit, if everyone had the chance to study my files, we'd soon be able to work out who was an informer, for example."

"Sure, but think of the upset. The anger."

"Macaulay, our little news sheet is usually rather dull. This would create huge waves. It's not something we can control. It could swamp us."

"Also, think of the shame, not to mention the unspeakable hurt, if the informer turns out to be, say, Edwin."

"Or Rafik. Even Billy."

"God, imagine the scandal if it proved to be Greta. Or Lenny Barr!"

"Sivuyile is convinced it's Marc Hendricks," declared Vogel, then muttered, "And vice versa."

"So far this is all personal resentments, prejudice and chitchat," sighed Zech. "But, really, have you given any thought to the absolute pandemonium we'd face if the culprit, after all, proved in fact to be Sivuyile Gqabe?"

"Let the cards fall where they may," replied Vogel stubbornly.

"People have been assassinated for less, *Bhuti*."

"And ..." Mary's voice faltered, became softer, almost inaudible, "Mac, what if the finger points at MB33?"

"Go on, we can say it. Say that name." Vogel breathed out, "Marda."

"Well?"

"Why is it that before, in opposition, we believed that the truth would set us free ... but now we are free at last, and in power, we quickly convince ourselves that it is the suppression of truth, in fact, which will keep us free?"

180

"I've a bad feeling about this," murmured Mary.

"It's too dangerous, Mac," agreed Zech. "You've signed on to state secrets, buddy."

"No, we're the problem," said Vogel with sudden vehemence. "We expected everyone to change, to be better people somehow. Instead, in our disappointment, it's we who've changed. But we don't want to admit this."

"No one will thank you, you know. Worst of all, there'll be no doubt about where we got your file. It'll whip up a vicious fuss, and there's no way we can disguise your information. Man, but you'll be thumped hard! People won't forgive you. You'll be insulted, called names - trouble-maker, agitator, conspirator. Maybe even *agent provocateur*. You'll become a public enemy and be hauled into court. Some might also claim you're trying to destabilise the new order, that you're a counter-revolutionary. Please, no. Believe me, old friend, I don't recommend it. You could go to jail for years."

Outside the distant mountain was beginning to lose its contours in the gathering dusk of an early winter's evening that stretched lengthy shadows over the room. Vogel sipped his whisky and surveyed the copies of both his files, next to each other, neatly collated on the dinning room table alongside a scattered disarray of pages that also spilled over onto chairs, sideboard and floor, sprinkled like petals after a storm. He felt relaxed and unexpectedly calm as he reflected that they would soon be assembled into an order and coherence that might begin make provisional sense of an unsolved world.

"Okay," Vogel agreed after a long silence. "I quite see your point."

His voice was confident and unexpectedly decisive. He was cheerful now that he'd made a decision. "I've only got one condition."

He indicated, on the table, the slim sheaves of neatly ordered papers, side by side, removed earlier from the unobtrusive lime green and stained beige folders: the photocopies of his own two files. "I want you to promise, should anything - absolutely anything - happen to me ... that you'll publish all those, both my personal Security Branch records, in *Umhlobo*."

It was almost dark by the time he left. A saffron glow smoldered over the mountain. He followed the curve back round the bay, delayed in heavy traffic. Vogel drove up Adderley Street and parked illegally outside the flower market. He ran across to the delicate, greying woman vendor from whom he had purchased flowers the previous week.

"What's your name?" he asked.

"Yusra," she replied.

"Yusra," the archivist marveled.

"Me, I'm always here. *Meneer* knows me."

"Yes, I do. Of course! Yusra ... absolutely. Thank you, Yusra. Listen, I'll take all the lilies you have left."

She clapped her hands. "But your wife, she's so lucky, she."

"No," said Vogel. "I'm the lucky one."

Twenty-five

MACAULAY VOGEL steps out; blinks against a mordant dazzle of wintery light. It's the shortest day. Moist air sparkles with sea-rinsed clarity. Sabata Dalindyebo Way - peach, apricot, his own mango yellow door - blushes under a topaz sun. He feels the languor of it on his face as he walks rapidly to work.

In Spin Street builders are already busy again on the construction site. Bulldozers, graders and mechanical diggers gouge out the earth and people hurry by without a glance.

He waits for lights to change at Darling Street, then strides diagonally across the Grand Parade. Amongst parked cars an all female township choir, uniform in virginal white, sings fervent hymns, ignored by stall holders and shoppers. Above them the plump marble figure of Edward VII continues to stare haughtily at the mock Renaissance grandeur of City Hall, its mature Bath limestone glowing creamily in the tender sunlight.

There's a bustle in the Castle courtyard. Tourists linger in lemon-clear sunshine. Seagulls caw overhead. Vogel breathes in cleansing ocean air.

He climbs the worn stone steps and sees, on the ramparts, a small gathering outside the storeroom next to his office. The door is open; the storeroom empty.

Onlookers fall silent. They gaze at the archivist. There are a dozen solders and civilians. He doesn't recognize anyone. Quickly Vogel fishes out his keys. He jiggles the key in the lock. The door to his office, however, will not open. He's flustered. He's aware of hushed scrutiny. He tries again and notices the latch has been secured with a padlock.

Two men wander over. He tries to pry open the padlock. They watch.

Vogel gives up. He looks round. The men have shaven heads and wear grey suits. He thinks at first they are the bodyguards he has seen before.

"Why is my office bolted?" asks Vogel.

"Inspector Appolis." The taller man holds out a hand. Vogel shakes it.

"Inspector Jansen," adds the other. He also shakes the archivist's hand.

"Why is my office bolted?" repeats Vogel.

"Dr. Vogel is it?"

"Dr. Macaulay Vogel?"

"Isak," replies Vogel. "My first name is Isak, in fact."

The men are surprised. Inspector Appolis consults a notebook.

"Inspector, why am I not able to access my office?"

"We have reason to believe, Dr. Vogel ..."

"You have appropriated state property."

"Confidential material," clarifies Appolis.

"Classified information," confirms Jansen.

They wait for him to reply. Vogel nods.

Appolis asks, "Do you have anything to say, Dr. Vogel?"

"Therefore thou art inexcusable, O man," recites the archivist, "whosoever thou art that judgest ..."

Appolis flicks open his notebook again. "Is this your statement?"

"For wherein thou judgest another, thou condemnst thyself - for thou that judgest doest the same things."

"You see," Jansen tells Appolis. "It's always the white guys who try to be funny. They think we can't touch them. White guys think they can get away with anything."

"Yup, that's the way of it," Appolis sighs.

The policeman extends his right hand again, palm upward. "*Meneer*, I must ask to see what you have in your shoulder bag."

Without hesitation, Vogel hands over his tattered old red duffel bag. Appolis unthreads the cords at the top and peers inside, then glances over meaningfully at Jansen. "I am going to have to ask you to come with us, sir."

Vogel turns round anxiously to see who may have overheard.

"This way please, sir. You will have to accompany us, Dr. Vogel."

Vogel hesitates. "What will happen to my files?"

"Whose?" Jansen snorts. "He thinks the documents belong to him!"

"Like the bones, sir," says Appolis. "They'll be taken somewhere safe."

They turn and the archivist follows. They pass the silent onlookers.

From the small crowd someone shouts, "Ask him about the bombs!"

The archivist cranes his neck to scan the crowd and spots Lieutenant Nxumalo, obscured at the back. Vogel catches his eye. Nxumalo shrugs.

Appolis goes down the steps first. The archivist follows. Jansen is in the rear. The Castle courtyard is peaceful. Vogel notices the grass is green and succulent after the winter rains. Some children are climbing on the cannons. Sunlight glows on his face. It seeps soothingly into his skin. He breathes in the aseptic sea breeze. He is calm. He feels, to his surprise, no anger. They pass through the arched entrance. Appolis and Jansen walk close to him, on either side. Their heavy shoes clatter on grey cobbles.

They emerge from the sheltered Castle gateway into sparkling sunshine again. Table Mountain rears up ahead, so clear Vogel feels he could reach out and touch the grizzled rock-face. He is astonished by this immaculate, midwinter lucidity. Never has he sensed the immensity of the mountain more forcefully; its immediate presence and beauty.

Cars are parked facing the Castle moat. A car guard with dreadlocks listens to music on headphones. He runs over to the unmarked police vehicle to claim his tip.

Jansen opens the back door for Vogel.

"You catch a bad guy?" asks the car guard.

"Yup," says Appolis and hands him a coin.

"*Eish*, you should lock up all the white guys."

Appolis drives. After fifty metres, they stop. Lights at Darling Street are red.

"*Kak*, man," says Jansen. He presses a switch. The police siren howls.

The sedan eases across the intersection and accelerates up Buitenkant. The siren is piercing. Vogel feels calm, even peaceful. Other cars move out of their path. In less than a minute they race by the College of Cape Town and, on the other side, a line of scruffy retail stores. They cross Caledon Street. The red-brick Magistrates' Court takes up the entire block. The car slows, turns into Albertus, skirting the side of the Magistrates' Court.

It is a quiet street, flanked by trees. Vogel sees a small gathering on the pavement. Hearing a siren, curious faces turn. People shake fists, shout. He cannot hear what they are yelling. The sedan glides by. Now he sees that the crowd is shouting at him. The sun slants obliquely. It shimmers through dense foliage, lacing petal-like patterns on the pavement.

"Betrayer, scum … criminal!"

He hears the enraged howls, sees angry faces through the rear window. These people whom he does not know are consumed with loathing for him, their yells pitiless with disgust. Two men with cameras give chase. Someone, thinks Vogel, must have tipped off the photographers, organized a crowd.

"Lock away the traitor!"

"Informer!"

"Spy!"

Catcalls and whistles are drowned out by an orchestrated chant of outraged rejection. Soon - perhaps tomorrow - how much more incensed will they be, he wonders, when the Xabas publish those rank, intolerable secrets?

The police car slowly swings into a tunneled side-entrance. It is dark. The sedan stops outside a thick wooden door. Vogel steps out. Jansen slips handcuffs onto his wrist. In the gloom, a camera flashes. Vogel blinks. He knows he looks guilty. Appolis and Jansen grasp the archivist's arms and march him through the medieval-looking door.

Yells of hatred grow fainter. The door closes. He is happy.